ARTHUR ASHE

Illustrated by Meryl Henderson

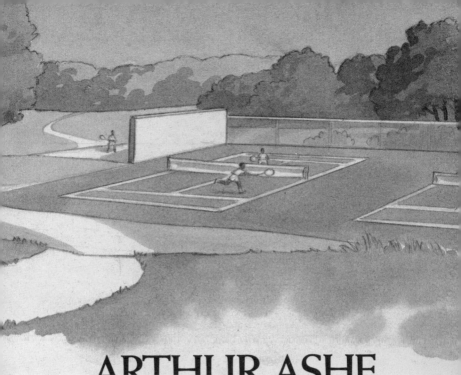

ARTHUR ASHE

Young Tennis Champion

by Paul Mantell

ALADDIN PAPERBACKS

New York   London   Toronto   Sydney

ALADDIN PAPERBACKS
An imprint of Simon & Schuster
Children's Publishing Division
1230 Avenue of the Americas
New York, NY 10020
Text copyright © 2006 by Paul Mantell
Illustrations copyright © 2006 by Meryl Henderson
All rights reserved, including the right of
reproduction in whole or in part in any form.
ALADDIN PAPERBACKS and colophon are trademarks of
Simon & Schuster, Inc.
CHILDHOOD OF FAMOUS AMERICANS is a registered trademark of
Simon & Schuster, Inc.
Designed by Lisa Vega
The text of this book was set in New Caledonia.
Manufactured in the United States of America
First Aladdin Paperbacks edition January 2006
2   4   6   8   10   9   7   5   3   1
Library of Congress Control Number 2005926078
ISBN-13: 978-0-689-87346-1
ISBN-10: 0-689-87346-3

ILLUSTRATIONS

CONTENTS

Big News

"Arthur Ashe Jr.! Come home this instant!"

Arthur heard his mother calling him from the upstairs window of the house across the street. She sounded annoyed.

He pretended not to hear her. He would come home, all right—just as soon as he was through playing tag. He wasn't worried that she'd be mad. She always forgave him when he did something wrong.

It was different with his father. If Mr. Ashe had been home, Arthur would have raced inside at once. But during the day his dad was never home. Mr. Ashe worked at many different jobs—chauffeur, gardener, carpenter—scraping together what little money he could. Back then, in 1947, that was how it was for most African-American men.

Arthur turned his attention back to the game. He was the fastest boy in the whole neighborhood, and everybody knew it. Small and thin and just four years old, he could outrun boys twice his age and size.

The only trouble was Arthur didn't get to run around very often. It seemed like he was always getting sick. He'd spent weeks in bed with measles, mumps, chicken pox, diphtheria, whooping cough, and who knew what else.

But he hadn't been sick now for almost a month. He felt fine, and that meant he was going to run around and play until he was good and tired of it—even if it did make his mother angry.

"Arthur!"

That was his father's voice!

Arthur Ashe Sr. was home, in the middle of the day—and he didn't like being ignored.

"Coming, Dad!"

Art crossed the street and ran inside the big house where he, his mom and dad, his baby brother, Johnnie, and lots of uncles, aunts, and cousins all lived. The house was near Brookfield Park, Richmond's largest playground for black people. Arthur rarely saw white people in the park. They didn't come around the neighborhood much at all.

Richmond, Virginia, the city where Arthur's family lived, had been the capital of the South, also called the Confederacy, during the Civil War. Along the city's main street there were still statues of Confederate Civil War heroes riding on horses, their swords raised to the sky. They had fought for slavery—but in Richmond they were still heroes.

Black Americans were no longer slaves by the 1940s. But in many ways things in the South—and in Richmond in particular—

hadn't changed very much by the time Arthur was a child.

In the South blacks and whites still lived apart. Blacks had to use separate restrooms, eat at different restaurants, sit in the backs of buses, live in separate neighborhoods, and go to separate schools and parks. The places set aside for blacks were never as nice as those for whites. Nowhere near as nice.

African Americans were called Negroes then, from the Spanish word for *black*. Some white people called them much worse names.

Southern Negroes lived in fear. Sometimes they were beaten up—or worse—for no reason at all except that they were black.

Arthur didn't pay much attention to any of this—he was still just a little boy. But one time, when his mother was pregnant with Johnnie, she took Art shopping downtown. There were no seats on the bus, so little Art asked a man to get up and let his mother sit.

4

The man was white. By law only whites could sit in the front section. But the man didn't get angry. He smiled and said, "Well, little boy, you've got spirit. Since you dared to ask me to get up and let your mama sit down, I'm going to do just that."

And he did.

Only years later did Arthur understand how unusual his courage had been. It was the first time Arthur Ashe Jr. showed the courage he was to display all his life.

Arthur's mother was waiting for him upstairs, in the room the four of them shared. Baby Johnnie sat in her lap. At the window stood Mr. Ashe with his arms folded across his chest.

"Didn't you hear me calling you, son?"

"Sure, Dad, but—"

"Don't 'but' me. Didn't you hear your *mother* calling you?"

"Um . . . I guess so."

"You guess so. When your mama calls you, you answer her, do you hear?"

6

"Yes, Dad."

"I don't want you running around like that," his mother said, looking anxious. "You'll get chilled and catch pneumonia."

"Now, Mattie," Mr. Ashe said. "Boys need to get exercise. It keeps them healthy."

Then Mr. Ashe turned to Arthur, who wondered if he was about to be punished. Instead his father asked him a surprising question.

"You're pretty fast, aren't you, son?"

"Yes, sir."

"Well, good. Because you're gonna have lots of room to run at our new house."

"Our . . . our new house?"

His father broke out into a big smile. Arthur leaped into his arms.

"I got a new job with the city of Richmond," Mr. Ashe told them all. "Special police officer. I'm going to be in charge of all of Brookfield Park!"

He pointed out the window, and they came over to look. The park was spread out before them. It had baseball fields, basketball courts, an Olympic-size swimming pool, tennis courts, and horseshoe pitches. They weren't in the best condition, but blacks in the South were happy to have any place to play at all.

"And right in the middle of the park is our new house!" Mr. Ashe said. "Five rooms! Isn't that something?"

"Oh, honey!" his wife said, her eyes glowing with happiness. "Finally a home of our own!"

"Five whole rooms of our own!" Art's father crowed.

Art knew the little house. It was right next to the tennis courts. He'd passed by it a hundred times and always wondered who lived there. Now it would be his and his family's!

"Just think, Mattie," Mr. Ashe said, his voice hushed. "Just think, Arthur—a home of our own!"

A Mother's Love

Every time he entered or left the new house, Arthur saw people playing tennis. He could look out his window at the courts and the nearby backboard, where you could hit the ball to yourself if you couldn't find anyone to play with.

Arthur wondered if he'd be any good at tennis. He was fast and athletic, and it did look like fun. Maybe someday he'd try it— when he was older and bigger and strong enough to swing a tennis racket really hard.

Art's favorite sport was definitely baseball.

Even at four years old he could throw and catch, and run the bases really well. He wasn't too good at hitting yet—the bats were all too heavy for him—but that would come in time.

The winds of change were blowing in America, even if they hadn't reached Richmond yet. It was 1947, the year Jackie Robinson became the first Negro player to play baseball in the major leagues. Until then Negroes had not been allowed to play with whites.

There were many white fans who didn't like Negroes, and they booed Robinson, even threatened to hurt him. But Robinson never answered back—even though deep down inside it must have hurt terribly.

In Art's neighborhood Robinson was everybody's hero. When Arthur played baseball, he wore an old T-shirt with the number forty-two drawn on it—Robinson's number. After playing ball, he would head back home through the park, imagining that someday he'd be a baseball star like Jackie Robinson.

Passing the tennis courts, he wondered if there was a Negro tennis star he could pretend to be. That night at dinner he asked his father about it.

Mr. Ashe frowned and shook his head. "No, son," he said. "Tennis is a white man's game."

"Then, how come we've got black folks playing right here?"

His father didn't answer, and Arthur could tell it would be a mistake to bother him about it anymore.

Still, in his own mind he tried to figure it out. If tennis was a white man's game, that could change, couldn't it? Jackie Robinson had changed baseball, hadn't he? And hadn't that been a white man's game too?

"Can't we read some more, Mama?" Arthur asked as she reached over to turn off the light.

She had taught him to read two years ago, at the age of four—before he had ever set foot in a school. From the very beginning he'd loved books. Magazines, too—*National Geographic* was his favorite. It made him want to travel all over the world someday and see everything there was to see.

"My word, Arthur, we've been reading for over an hour! Aren't you sleepy yet?"

"Nuh-uh. Besides, I was only reading half that time. The rest of the time you were reading to me."

His mother laughed. Then she bent over and kissed him, although it was difficult now because her belly was so big. She said good night and left the room, turning off the light.

A while back she had told Art and Johnnie that there was going to be a new baby in the family. Then a month ago she'd let them feel how the baby moved around in her belly. Arthur was excited about having a new brother or sister.

Lately, though, he had become more and

more worried about his mom. She didn't look good. Her ankles were terribly swollen, and she was tired all the time. Arthur could tell that his dad was worried too, although Mr. Ashe never said anything about it.

Art looked over at Johnnie, who was snoring peacefully. He wished he could sleep too. But he kept thinking of all those times he'd wandered off when his mom had called for him to come home.

Once, the summer before, he'd gotten lost and didn't find his way home till long after dark. When he did, he discovered that all the neighbors had been out looking for him. His mom said she'd been "worried sick."

Arthur wondered if that was why she was sick now. Why, oh, why hadn't he come when she'd called him?

Tomorrow she would be going to the hospital for a "procedure." Art didn't know what a procedure was, and no one seemed to want to tell him anything about it. All he knew was he had the best mother in the world, and he would try never to disappoint her again.

A day went by, and his mother did not return from the hospital. His father came home late that evening, looking sadder than Art had ever seen him.

"There were complications after the surgery," he said.

"Is she going to be all right, Dad?"

For a moment his father didn't answer. Then he said, "I have faith she will be. Now, you go pray for her, and get to bed."

Another day went by and another, and still Arthur's mother did not come home. Each night when he returned from the hospital, Mr. Ashe looked sadder and wearier than the day before.

Still, Arthur was sure that his mother would be better soon. Hadn't his father said to have faith?

A few nights later Art and Johnnie were lying in bed with the lights out. Art thought

Johnnie must be asleep, he was so quiet. So Arthur began to pray out loud—softly.

"Dear God, please let Mama get well. Please don't let her die. I'm sorry for whenever I was bad to her or made her cry." He felt tears welling up in his own eyes as he spoke.

"Mama gonna die?" Johnnie suddenly piped up, his little voice sounding scared.

"No, silly. Moms don't die."

"You said 'don't let her die.'"

Art caught his breath. "I was just . . . saying that."

"Why?"

"Well, because I was praying. That's how you talk when you pray."

"Oh." Johnnie didn't sound convinced, but he soon drifted off back to sleep.

The next morning the boys were awoken by the sound of their father crying his eyes out. Mr. Ashe burst into the room, came over to their bunk bed, and held them tightly to him, one boy in each arm.

"What is it, Dad?" Art asked, afraid to hear the answer.

"Where's Mama?" Johnnie blurted out.

Mr. Ashe caught his breath. Tears streamed down his face.

"She's gone to heaven," he said, his voice shaking with sobs. "You boys are all I've got left . . . all I've got left . . . all I've got left. . . ."

Alone in the World

Her family, friends, and fellow church members brought Mattie Ashe home to lay her out for burial. They dressed her up in her Sunday best and put makeup on her face.

Her heart had always been weak, and the problems with her pregnancy had caused her to have a stroke. In the end her heart had simply given out.

People came and went all day and evening, and the next day too. They brought cakes and pies, and casseroles and flowers, and they brought the cold March air into the house when they came and went. They shuffled into the parlor to see Mattie Ashe for the last time.

Arthur was still too scared to be near her. His mother was dead now, he knew. But she didn't *look* dead, only very still and quiet.

That night before bed, when all the relatives and friends and strangers were gone, he padded into the living room on tiptoe. "Good-bye, Mama," he whispered, and kissed her cold cheek. Then he backed out of the room, taking one last, long look.

He was shaking all over by the time he got upstairs. "Dad," he told his father, "I don't want to go to the funeral."

"What?" his father said, his eyes widening.

"I can't stand to see Mama like that anymore."

Mr. Ashe sighed, looked down at the floor, and took Arthur's hand. "It's all right, son," he said. "You don't have to go if you don't want to. Just be a good boy. Always. That's what she wanted you to be."

"I will be." Art meant it too. He would make his mother, and his father, proud of him. Always.

He watched from a neighbor's yard the next morning as the funeral procession marched away through Brookfield Park, carrying his mother in her coffin. The kids playing basketball on the nearby courts all stood still and bowed their heads.

The sad music of a brass band faded into the distance with the funeral parade. Arthur wiped away his tears and went back into the house.

Everywhere around the living room were pictures of his mother, put there for visiting friends and family to see. But they were only pictures—they were not his mom!

The house was much too quiet. Arthur went back outside and wandered over toward the tennis courts.

It was March, but warm enough for some hardy souls to come out and play. On the far court were two young people hitting the ball to each other. The near court was empty, but Arthur saw a pair of rackets lying under a bench, with a couple of balls next to them.

Maybe the owners had gone off to get some lunch from the hot dog truck at the other end of the park.

Art knew he shouldn't touch other people's things, but he was curious. He picked up one of the rackets, held it in his two bony hands like it was a baseball bat, and swung as hard as he could.

Swoosh! He heard the wind whistle through the racket's strings. He liked the sound of it and tried it again, and again and again.

Looking around, he still didn't see anybody. The couple on the far court didn't seem to notice him. There was nobody using the backboard, which was hidden from their view.

What harm could it do? he thought.

Arthur bent down and picked up one of

the tennis balls. He would return everything before anyone noticed. He walked quickly over to the backboard, bounced the ball once or twice, then hit it against the wall.

Thwack!

It came back to him, and he swung at it, missing badly. But that didn't stop him. He hit the ball again—and this time he was ready.

Ten minutes later he was still hitting the ball against the wall. By now he was getting good at it. He liked the feeling of whacking the ball as hard as he could, over and over again. It made some of the sad feelings about his mom's death go away.

"Hey, you—kid!" A man's angry voice rang out from the direction of the tennis courts. "Give me back my racket!"

Arthur panicked. He dropped the racket and ran away as fast as he could. The man didn't chase him; he only picked up his racket and ball and went back to the courts.

Arthur hid behind a tree trunk until the

man and his tennis partner had finished playing and left the area. Only then did he go
back to his house.

It had been a narrow escape, but Arthur
didn't feel afraid. He had found a new, exciting sport to play. As soon as his father got
home from the funeral, Art decided, he was
going to ask him for a tennis racket.

Instead of a racket Arthur got a very unpleas-
ant surprise. "You two boys are going to go
spend some time with your aunt and uncle,"
Mr. Ashe told them.

"I don't want to go!" little Johnnie wailed.

Arthur held back his tears. He had done his
crying in private, and he wasn't about to act like
a little child now. He was six years old, after
all—old enough to understand that his father
was hurting and needed his sons to be strong.

"How long will we be there, Dad?" he
asked.

"I'm not sure," Mr. Ashe said. "Not too

long, I hope. Right now I just can't take care of you boys and still do my job for the city."

"It's okay, Dad. We'll be good."

"That's my boy," said Mr. Ashe. He hugged both his sons tightly. "That's my two good boys."

"When Daddy gonna come?" Johnnie asked Arthur.

They had been at their relatives' house in central Virginia for quite a while now. Art wasn't sure how long. A few months probably, but it felt like years.

Every time their dad came to visit, the boys would beg him to take them home with him. "Not yet," he would tell them.

It got longer and longer between visits, and Art was beginning to think they would always live here. Even if they did go home soon, it would never be the same without their mom.

"I don't know when, Johnnie," Art said. "And quit asking me, will you?"

Finally the great day came. Their father announced that he was taking them back to Richmond with him. Both boys were over-joyed—but Art wasn't going to make a big scene about it. He was almost seven now. Too grown up to jump up and down like baby Johnnie.

Besides, Art had learned not to get too excited about anything. You never knew when something bad would happen and all your happiness would go away in an instant. Like with his mother. When she died, it was like a beautiful bubble had burst.

Sure enough, they were only halfway back to Richmond when their father announced: "I need help raising you, what with my job and all. So I've decided you boys need a new mother."

"You getting married again, Dad?" Art asked, astonished.

"No. Mrs. Berry is an older lady who's going to be living with us from now on."

"What about her husband?" Art asked.

"Her husband died, son."

"Didn't she have any children of her own?"

"Yes, she did. But they're all grown up now and on their own."

Mr. Ashe cleared his throat and went on. "Mrs. Berry will be doing the housekeeping, but I want you boys to understand that she is more than just a housekeeper. She is there to be a mother to you—and you're to call her Mother. Understood?"

Three-year-old Johnnie nodded his head, looking confused. But Art understood perfectly—and he didn't like it one bit. He already *had* a mother, even if she was dead. No one else would *ever* be his mother—no one ever *could* be!

Mrs. Berry was waiting for them when they arrived back at the house in Brookfield Park. She was standing just outside the doorway, waving and smiling, and calling, "Hello!"

26

"Dad," Art said, "how *old* is she?"

"We don't ask that kind of question, son. It's rude."

"But she looks so *old*!"

"Never mind that, Arthur. Now, you be respectful."

"Yes, sir."

Arthur walked up to Mrs. Berry and stood there, next to his brother.

His father said, "Boys, this is Mrs. Berry. She's going to be living with us from now on."

"Hi," Johnnie said cheerfully, but Arthur just looked at his shoes. He wasn't a baby like Johnnie. He knew what was going on.

"Now, I want you boys to mind Mrs. Berry and be respectful," Mr. Ashe went on. "I promised her that if she came to live with us, she would be the boss of the house. The Ashes honor their promises. We're all going to listen to what Mrs. Berry says—and that includes me."

Art couldn't believe his ears. His father had always been the boss of the house. He was the boss of the whole park! How could he let this old lady boss all of them around?

"Now, come on in, everyone, and let's celebrate," Mr. Ashe said. "I've got ice cream—I know how much you boys like ice cream!"

"I'm . . . I'm not hungry," Art said.

"What?" Mr. Ashe could scarcely believe it.

"I don't feel too well. May I be excused? I'd like to go to bed."

"All right, son," Mr. Ashe said, looking puzzled. "I hope you're all right. We'll save you some for when you feel better."

Arthur went up the stairs, feeling everyone's eyes on him.

"Now, Arthur," Mr. Ashe whispered in his son's ear. In the bottom bunk bed little Johnnie lay asleep, softly snoring. "I want you to call Mrs. Berry 'Mother' from now on."

"I won't!" Arthur whispered. "She's not my mother, and I won't call her that."

"No, she's not your mother—but she's *a* mother. And you boys need someone to care for you like a mother. I can't do that, no matter how hard I try."

"But Mrs. Berry's so *old*!"

"Old people know an awful lot, Arthur. They've been around a long time, and if they're wise, like Mrs. Berry, they come to know things. We should all listen to her and respect her."

"But—"

"That's enough now, son," Mr. Ashe said, getting up to go. "Good night."

"Dad?"

"Yes?"

"Leave the door open a little, all right?"

Arthur soon found that his father was right about Mrs. Berry. She was pretty smart, and she had a good, sly sense of humor. When Arthur was rude or mean to her (as he often was in the beginning), she didn't get mad at him. Instead she'd say something totally unexpected, like "Arthur, you just make sure you can hold your head high and always be proud of yourself."

It made him realize that he really wanted to be respectful, so that people would respect him back. He noticed that his own father, the man he looked up to more than any other, was always respectful and obedient to Mrs. Berry.

Mrs. Berry was tough on Art and Johnnie, true, but she also stuck up for them when Mr. Ashe was being unfair. "These boys are good boys," she would tell him. "You've got no call to be mad at them."

Still, Arthur wished she weren't living with them. One night when his father had to work late, and Mrs. Berry was serving the boys dinner, Arthur was in a particularly bad mood. Pushing away his plate, he told Mrs. Berry, "I hate the way you cook. Your food is bad!"

Mrs. Berry stood very still for a moment.

Arthur thought she was going to yell at him. To his surprise, she gave him a sad smile instead. "Well, Arthur, I'm sure the good Lord will reward you for putting up with my poor cooking." Then she turned and went slowly into the kitchen.

Arthur felt terrible. He had wanted to make Mrs. Berry angry, but every time he said something nasty to her, she replied to him with kind words. He realized that she was doing her best to raise him the right way. For the first time he felt lucky to have her living with them.

He followed her into the kitchen. "I'm sorry," he said. "I didn't mean it."

She patted him on the shoulder. "That's all right, Arthur. I know you didn't."

A New Friend and Teacher

The days were lonely for Arthur. He didn't care much about school anymore, and his grades began to get worse. He still loved playing baseball, but most of the time the fields were taken up by the bigger kids.

So he took to spending a lot of time sitting in his room, reading the books and magazines he and his mother had read together.

Often he'd look out his window at the tennis courts. Arthur wished he could play that game. It looked like so much fun—especially the way Ronald Charity played it.

Ronald Charity was a young man working his way through Virginia Union College, a school for Negroes. Arthur knew his name because everyone around the tennis courts was always talking about him. Ronald Charity was the best tennis player any of them had ever seen.

When the weather was good, Art would go outside and sit beside the tennis courts and backboard, watching Charity hit the ball. The young man didn't seem to notice him, he was so busy concentrating.

One night Arthur found his father's old tennis racket tucked away at the back of the hall closet. It had a cloth cover with a pocket, and inside the pocket was an old tennis ball.

Arthur was so excited he could hardly speak. He knew he should ask his father's permission to use it, but what if his dad said no?

The next morning, a Saturday, Art got up early. He wanted to get out to the backboard and claim it before anyone else did. The rules

34

of the park were that whoever was playing on the backboard had a right to stay there until he or she was done.

Art hadn't hit a tennis ball except for that one time, the day of his mom's funeral. But it didn't take him long to remember how. The only trouble was every time he hit a shot too high, it would go over the top of the back-board, and he'd have to run through the gate in the fence that surrounded the courts, and around behind them, to retrieve his one and only ball.

One time an older boy and girl came through the gate just as Arthur was getting his ball. By the time he returned to the back-board, the boy and girl had already begun playing!

"Hey!" he shouted at them. "I was here first!"

"There was nobody here," the boy said.

"I was just getting my ball back there," Art said, pointing.

"Yeah, well, get lost, kid!"

"I will not!"

They started yelling back and forth at each other. Arthur lost his temper and called the boy a bad name. Then both the boy and the girl chased him all through the park. Luckily, Art was so fast that not many people could keep up with him. The boy and girl finally gave up.

Unluckily, they reported the incident to Arthur's father—the officer in charge of the park.

When Art got home, his father was waiting for him in the living room.

"I had a serious complaint about you, son," he said.

"I was there first!" Art argued. "Those are the rules!"

"Those people said you sassed them."

"I did not!"

His father gave him a long look. "You real-ize that your word is precious? That it is all you really have in this life?"

"Yes, Dad. I know."

"And you give me your word you didn't sass them."

Art thought for a moment. He decided that he hadn't sassed them—he'd simply stood up for his rights. He had been there first, hadn't he? "Yes, sir," he said.

"All right, then. I'll accept your word, Arthur. But don't let me hear about anything like this happening again. Next time you want to argue with somebody in this park, you come to me about it first. Remember, I'm the one in charge here. And you're my son."

"Yes, Dad. Oh, and Dad?"

"Yes?"

"May I still use your tennis racket?"

Mr. Ashe smiled. "Yes, you may. Just as long as you play by the rules and act like a gentleman."

The next day Arthur sat courtside, watching Ronald Charity hit the ball against the backboard. Art had his racket and ball with him, just in case. Charity noticed.

"Hey, there!" he called.

Art pointed to himself. "Me?"

"Yes, you. What's your name, kid?"

"Arthur Ashe Jr."

"I'm Ronald Charity." They shook hands. "Your dad runs the park, right?"

"Yes, sir."

"I see you've got yourself a racket, huh?"

"It's my dad's." Arthur held it up to show him.

"It's way too big and heavy for you. Are you sure you're strong enough to swing it?"

"Sure am!" Art said proudly. "Watch!"

He threw his only tennis ball high in the air and took a mighty, two-handed swing at it. The ball sailed over the backboard, landing out of sight far, far away.

Charity looked surprised. "Wow! How much do you weigh, Arthur? Sixty pounds at most, I'll bet."

Art shrugged. He wasn't sure how much he

weighed. But what difference did it make?

"I'm amazed you can hit the ball that hard and that far."

Arthur beamed with pride.

"But you hit it like it was a baseball. There are no home runs in tennis. You have to stroke the ball, not just whack it."

"Huh?"

Charity looked down at him, scratching his chin thoughtfully. "I'm going to be teaching tennis here this summer," he said. "But I think you're a little young for lessons."

"No! Teach me, please!" Art begged. "I'm big enough—I can hit it really hard. You said so yourself!"

"I've done some impossible things in my time," Charity said. "Taught myself tennis from a book—that wasn't easy. But teaching a six-year-old to play? I don't think so."

"I'm seven!"

"Seven, huh?" Charity frowned.

"Well, I'll be seven on July tenth."

"I see. Still, you're small for your age. Well, I'll tell you what. Let's try a quick lesson right now and see how you do."

"Right now?"

"Right now."

Art was so excited he didn't know what to say. He just followed Charity onto the tennis courts—the real ones, not the backboard.

"Now first, let me show you how to hold the racket," Charity said. "It's called the grip."

He showed Art how to line his hand up with the handle of the racket, fitting it into his palm. The racket *was* too big for him, as Charity had said. But somehow he managed to get his hand into something like the proper grip.

"Good," said Charity. "Now go over to the other side of the net, Arthur. I'll hit you some shots, and you hit the ball back to me, okay?"

Art did as he was told. Charity hit him a ball to his right, and Art wound up and hit it back sharply.

"Good!" Charity said. "Let's try it again."

The second shot came at him, and Arthur hit it back hard again, but this time he hit it too high.

"Swing straight back at hip level, then straight forward," Charity told him. Arthur hit the next five shots perfectly.

"You're a fast learner!" Charity complimented him, and Arthur could feel himself swelling up with pride.

"That shot is called a forehand. It's great when the other guy hits it to your right—but what are you going to do if he hits it on the other side of you?"

Arthur stood there, wishing he knew the answer.

"Here, I'll show you. It's called a backhand, and you have to change your grip to hit it. Here, move your thumb like this. Now turn to your left and swing through. Yes! Good one!"

No matter what Charity told him to do,

Arthur was able to do it easily and quickly. "You're gonna be fun to teach!" Charity told him, ruffling Art's hair.

Two men with rackets came over to them. "Excuse me, we've got the court for ten o'clock," one of them said.

"Give us five more minutes," Charity told them.

"Aw, come on, he's just a kid," the second man said, looking at Arthur. "You can't hog the court to play with a little kid."

"Just watch him," Charity told them.

And they did. For the next ten minutes Art and Ronald Charity hit the ball back and forth while the two men watched.

"How old's this kid?" the first man asked.

"I'm seven," Art replied.

"Seven! Incredible."

"He's actually still six," Charity said. "And it's his first time on a tennis court."

"Whoa! Hey, kid, you're gonna be great at this game—keep it up!"

Art and Charity walked off the court together.

"Did I do okay?" Art asked, even though he knew the answer.

"You did fine," Charity said. "How about I give you lessons this summer?"

"Oh, I'd like that!" Arthur said. "But . . . I don't think my dad can afford it."

"Well, I'll tell you what," said Charity. "This first summer I'll teach you for free, and in exchange you help me out with my other students—you know, fetch the tennis balls and stuff. Sound good to you?"

"You bet!" Arthur said, and ran home to tell Mrs. Berry and his father the good news. Not only did he have a tennis coach, he had made a new friend.

Even more important, he had a new favorite game—tennis.

It's How You Play the Game

All through that summer of 1950, Art spent more time on the tennis court than he did on the baseball field.

Charity taught him all the different kinds of shots—serves, passing shots, volleys, cross-court shots, lobs. He taught him how to hit the ball with topspin, backspin, and no spin at all. He showed Art how to run up to the net so you could hit the ball before it bounced, and how to serve with a hard smash or a soft cut shot.

Soon everyone around the tennis courts of

Brookfield Park knew who Arthur Ashe Jr. was. But that didn't mean they liked him. In fact, Arthur soon had himself a new nickname: the Pest.

Whenever he wasn't taking up court time with Ronald Charity, he was hogging the backboard, hitting the ball to himself over and over again.

There were only four tennis courts in Brookfield Park, and far too many players wanted to use them. Many of them were annoyed that a seven-year-old kid always seemed to be there before them and never wanted to leave.

"First come, first served," he would tell them.

Arthur didn't care about being called a pest. For the first time since his mother had died, he was happy. He and Mrs. Berry were getting along much better, and his new friend, Mr. Charity, was teaching him tennis.

Toward the end of the summer he told his father how happy he was. "Someday," he said, "I'm gonna be better at tennis than Mr. Charity and better at baseball than Jackie Robinson!"

"That's good, Arthur," Mr. Ashe said. "I'm glad you have big dreams. It's fine to want to be the best at something, and baseball and tennis are fine sports. But just remember, sports aren't everything."

"I know that, Dad."

"There are many more important things in life," Mr. Ashe went on. "Like studying and reading and helping others."

"Yes, Dad."

"Very few people make money playing sports. To have a good career, you need a good education. If you want to spend lots of time getting better at sports, that's all right with me—so long as you promise to study hard this year and get good grades."

"I will, Dad!" Arthur promised. He wanted

to do well in school, and not just to please his father. Arthur was starting to take pride in himself and in everything he did. Even more important, he wanted to be the sort of boy that his mother would have been proud of.

It was a good year at school for Arthur, and both his father and Mrs. Berry were pleased with him. He still felt sad about his mother sometimes, and he thought about her nearly every day. But he was getting used to life without her. He had even started calling Mrs. Berry "Mother," as his father had asked him to.

He did very well at school. Arthur had always been an intelligent, thoughtful boy, and now that he was paying attention in class, his grades were excellent.

After school he was not allowed to go off and play with the other boys, who were "hanging out" in the park. He had to help his father with a thousand things, to take care of Brookfield Park.

Art and Johnnie learned a lot about park maintenance. "Pretty soon you boys'll be able to take over this job yourselves!" Mr. Ashe said proudly.

There were lots of chores to do. Art and Johnnie would often gather wood that had fallen from the trees and chop it up for firewood. That way the Ashes wouldn't have to spend too much money for heat in the winter.

Arthur and his family went to church every Sunday, just as they had before his mother's death. The church members were like part of a great big family. Most of them were just like his dad and Mrs. Berry—fine, upstanding people who were struggling to get by in a world that was very unkind to black people.

Being a part of that big family, Arthur learned many important lessons about life. He learned that it was important always to do the right thing, no matter how he felt about it. He learned to treasure his friends and family, and to care for the poor and the sick.

And he learned that no matter how badly you were treated because of the color of your skin, it was wrong to "get people back."

As the next summer drew near, Arthur was looking forward to more time with Ronald Charity on the tennis courts. His father had agreed to pay for lessons and had even bought him a used tennis racket that was more Art's size.

His days that summer were scheduled tightly, just like they were when he was at school. In the mornings he played baseball with his friends. He wore his favorite T-shirt—the one his mother had let him draw Jackie Robinson's number forty-two on—even though it was getting to be too small for him.

Then he would go swimming in Brookfield Park's pool before going home for a quick lunch. After that it was on to the tennis courts, where he would spend hours practicing with Mr. Charity on the courts and by himself at the backboard.

One day around Arthur's birthday, July 10, Charity said, "You know, Art, you're really improving. I'm so pleased with your progress that I'm considering entering you in the tournament. What do you think about that?"

"The tournament? Wow!"

Arthur didn't need to be told which tournament—there was only one each year in Brookfield Park. Boys and girls of all ages up to eighteen signed up to compete.

"I'm gonna win that trophy," Arthur said.

Mr. Charity laughed and patted his shoulder. "Well, that's good, Arthur," he said. "I'm glad you've got the spirit of competition. Just remember, most of these players are much older and bigger than you. Don't be disappointed if you lose this first time around."

"I'm not gonna lose. I'm gonna win," Arthur said, sure of himself.

"I'm sure you will, someday," Mr. Charity said, leaving it at that. "Just remember—it's not whether you win or lose, it's how you play the game. That's the most important thing."

Arthur wasn't listening, though. He was busy imagining himself hoisting that trophy over his head.

From the first day he'd swung a racket, Arthur had been dying to get into a real game of tennis. At first Mr. Charity wouldn't let him—not until he'd mastered the rules of the game and all the shots he needed to learn. Only then did he let Arthur have his wish. They would play a set, where the first player to win six games is the winner. Charity would let Arthur win sometimes—but not always. He wanted the little boy to understand that you couldn't win every time.

Arthur soon realized that Mr. Charity was letting him win, and he didn't like it. "I can beat you fair and square," he said.

"You think so?"

"Well, no," Art admitted. "Not yet. But someday."

"I'm sure you're right," Charity told him, patting him on the shoulder. "You just keep on practicing, and you'll get there—sooner than you think."

The tennis matches in Brookfield Park's tournament were won by taking two out of three sets. Arthur's first match went well. He was much more talented than the boy he was playing against. He won the first set, six games to one.

Early in the second set he made a dazzling shot that sent the other boy falling to the ground. Pleased with himself, Arthur looked around to see who was watching. He liked seeing the amazed looks on all the people's faces. They couldn't believe such a little boy like him was playing so well.

Then he saw Ronald Charity's face. Mr. Charity wasn't smiling. Not at all. Arthur wondered why he looked so angry.

When the match was over, he found out.

Arthur finished his opponent off, two sets

to none, waved to the applauding crowd, and walked over to his coach.

"I won!" he said proudly.

Charity didn't shake his hand or congratulate him. Instead he said, "Come with me—I want to talk to you."

He led Arthur through the gate and out into the park. "I don't ever want to see that kind of behavior from you again."

"What kind of behavior?" Art asked, stung by his friend's angry words.

"Showing off like that. It's rude and mean. How do you think that other boy felt when you did that?"

Arthur tried to put himself in the other boy's place. He saw what Mr. Charity was talking about. "Sorry," he said, and he meant it too. "I won't do it again."

"I hope not," Charity said. "You're much too good to be behaving like that. Bragging is bad behavior—if you do it again, I won't ever give you another lesson. Understand?"

Arthur nodded. He had felt so good just a minute ago. Now he felt lower than a worm.

His next match, the following day, was against a boy three years older than himself. Arthur played well and even won the second set after losing the first. But in the end the other boy was just too much bigger and stronger. Arthur lost the match in three sets.

He shuffled off the court, feeling terrible. It had never occurred to him that he might lose. Now he would never get that trophy he'd wanted so badly.

He felt like throwing his racket to the ground, but he knew what Mr. Charity would say. Worse, his father would be furious.

To Art's surprise, Mr. Charity didn't look mad at him—not at all. He knelt down and gave Art a big hug and said, "I'm proud of you, kid. You were fantastic."

"I was?"

"You gave that kid all he could handle,"

Charity said. "It was amazing. You almost had him beat—and he's eleven years old!"

"But I lost," Art said, sighing miserably.

"Never mind," Mr. Charity said. "There'll be other tournaments. Sooner or later you're going to win your share. Just remember, Arthur—it's not whether you win or lose, it's how you play the game."

He'd heard those words before, but until now he hadn't really paid attention. Now Arthur began to understand what they meant.

Yesterday he'd won the match, but he'd lost his coach's respect. Today he'd lost, but Mr. Charity was proud of him.

He was beginning to understand that tennis was more than just a game.

Trials and Triumphs

The next summer took forever to arrive. Finally school ended for the year, and Art was free to spend all day playing baseball and tennis.

During the year he'd gotten a little bigger—and a lot better.

Every shot that Ronald Charity taught him, Arthur learned quickly and well. He could make pretty much all the different shots now. His backhand and serve were getting stronger, catching up with his forehand. Art could now hit the ball as hard as a grown-up.

The smaller racket helped too. Art found he could swing it harder than the old, heavier one. This one was still too big for him—at least, Mr. Charity said so—but it was the best he could do for now.

Arthur grew even more excited as the annual Brookfield Park tournament drew nearer. He meant to win this year. He knew he had gotten much better at the game.

Over the spring and summer Mr. Charity had been taking him to other tournaments, at other Negro parks in Richmond. Arthur hadn't won any trophies yet, but he'd played well and won a lot of matches against older, bigger boys along the way.

Mr. Charity had also taken him a few times to the Richmond Racquet Club, where he played against adults, improving his game.

He felt sure now that he could win the Brookfield Park tournament. The boy who'd beaten him in the finals last year was now too old to be in the junior division. Even if he'd had to face him again, Arthur felt sure he could have beaten him.

He practiced harder than ever, hogging the backboard, annoying the older players who wanted to use it. But he didn't care. He wanted to win that tournament more than anything.

Mr. Charity kept telling him, "Remember, there are lots of older, bigger boys competing, and you might not win. Don't forget, winning isn't everything."

Art knew that. Of course he did. But he couldn't help feeling that if he wanted it badly enough, nothing could stop him. It was a feeling of confidence he would carry with him his whole career.

One day, three weeks before the tournament, he finished his morning game of baseball early. He decided to take a ride through the park on his bicycle—something he did whenever he had time to kill before his tennis lesson.

He sped through the park, dodging children and grown-ups who were blocking the path. Finally he decided to avoid the path altogether and just ride over the grass and through the trees. He did wheelies, skidding to a stop as he turned his bike to one side. He did jumps and quick turns, one after the other.

"Yeah! That was fun!" he said as he turned his bike around and headed for home. It was time for his tennis lesson.

He was almost there now, racing at top speed because he didn't want to be late. He never saw the big crack in the walkway until his wheel caught in it, stopping his bike cold.

Art flew over the handlebars and through the air. He reached out one arm to break his fall and came down hard on it.

"Owwww!" he cried as he hit the ground.

He lay there for a minute, then tried to get up—and couldn't.

His shoulder screamed out in pain. He couldn't turn his head.

"Mother!" he shouted, walking toward the house.

Mrs. Berry came outside. She saw how he was walking and ran to his side.

"Arthur, what happened?" she asked.

"I . . . fell . . . off my bike. . . ."

"Come on inside. I'm calling the doctor."

"No! I've got my tennis lesson!"

"Never mind that. You come with me, right this instant."

The doctor felt Art's shoulder and nodded his head slowly. "I'm afraid you've broken your collarbone, young man," he said.

"What?"

He had been sick plenty of times, but he'd never broken a bone before. Still, he knew plenty of kids who had. He knew that it took them a month before they even had their casts taken off.

"Do I have to have a cast?" he asked the doctor.

"You have to go to the hospital, son," the

doctor said. "You'll be there for a while, too. But don't worry—you'll live."

"But . . . what about tennis? And baseball?" Art wanted to know.

"Oh, you'll play them again," the doctor assured him. "But not for a good long while."

Oh, no! Art thought. *What about the tournament?*

How was he going to play in it now?

In those days people stayed in the hospital much longer than they do today. Arthur's doctor told him he'd be there for three weeks, and even then his shoulder wouldn't be fully healed. It would take at least six weeks for that—and the tournament would be over and done with by then.

Arthur was miserable. Ronald Charity came to see him and tried to cheer him up. Maybe there would be a miracle, he said. Maybe Arthur would heal in time for the tournament.

But even Charity never thought Arthur

would heal as fast as he did. In only two weeks he was out of the hospital, and he told Charity that he was going to play in the tournament, no matter what.

Charity wasn't so sure. Even if Arthur felt well enough—even if his doctor said it was okay—he'd still be going into the tournament with no chance to practice.

Three days later Art was back on the tennis court. His neck was stiff and his shoulder hurt him when he twisted certain ways, but he refused to let that stop him.

Ronald Charity had never seen such determination—certainly not from a nine-year-old boy. Arthur Ashe had always been a quick learner, but now Charity saw that he had something else as well—the heart of a champion.

In his first match of the tournament Arthur easily beat his much bigger, older opponent. The next day he beat another older boy.

Everyone was starting to take notice. Each day larger and larger crowds surrounded the tennis courts of Brookfield Park. Everyone wanted to see the skinny little boy who was tearing up the tournament.

Arthur kept on winning, day after day, until he made it to the final match. The other boy was almost twelve years old and much taller than Arthur. Surely, everyone thought, this boy would finish off young Ashe's remarkable run.

Mrs. Berry was there to watch, holding Johnnie's hand. Arthur Ashe Sr. was there too. He hadn't wanted Art to play because he thought he might hurt his shoulder again. But Mrs. Berry had said Arthur could play if he felt well enough—and Mr. Ashe had promised to obey Mrs. Berry.

With nearly every shot Arthur swung his racket so hard that he came clean off the ground. The ball blazed off his racket like a bullet. The older boy was a good tennis player—he had beaten everyone else with ease—but Arthur was too much for him.

When the match was over, a roar went up from the crowd. The tournament's sponsor hung a medal around Art's neck and shook his hand.

Arthur couldn't believe it. Two weeks ago he had been lying in a hospital bed. Now he was the new junior tennis champion of Brookfield Park!

Now What?

After the excitement was over and all the people had left, Art sat there on a bench with Ronald Charity.

Art looked at his medal for the thousandth time. It shone in the sun like it was made of gold. It wasn't, but that was okay. It was *his,* and that meant he was a champion.

"I'm proud of you, Arthur," Charity said.

"Thanks."

"I think you could be a really good tennis player someday."

That surprised Arthur. He thought he was

already a good player. What did Mr. Charity mean?

"Arthur, have you ever thought about what you want to do when you grow up?"

"Huh?"

"I mean, are you going to take over for your father here in the park, or do you have other plans?"

Art thought about it. "I want to be a baseball player," he said.

He had been playing a lot of ball the past two summers and was getting to be a really good fielder. He still couldn't hit the ball very far—not like he could hit a tennis ball, anyway. But baseball had been his dream ever since Jackie Robinson showed it was possible for Negroes to play in the major leagues.

"Baseball, huh?" Charity said, nodding. "Ever think about a future in tennis?"

Arthur hadn't. "I like tennis," he said, "but there aren't any major leagues, are there?"

"Well, no, there aren't—not yet," Charity said. "Maybe there will be someday."

"Well, what can you do in tennis, then?"

"Well, you can play in matches and tournaments. You could even go to college on a tennis scholarship and play on your college team."

"My dad says tennis is a white man's game. If there's a major league someday, you think they'll let black folks play in it?"

"I do," Charity said, and nodded. "You ever hear of Althea Gibson?"

Arthur hadn't.

"She's one of the best women players in the world right now. She's the ATA women's champion."

"What's the ATA?"

"American Tennis Association. It's for Negroes."

"Do they let her play in the white folks' tournaments?"

"Well, not in this country. The USLTA— that's the United States Lawn Tennis

Association—they mostly don't let black folks play. Not in the South, anyway, and definitely not here in Richmond. Still, she's going to play in England next year, at Wimbledon. And I'll bet you she wins, too! She's one of the best women players ever."

"What's Wimbledon?"

"Wimbledon? It's the oldest, biggest, most important tennis tournament in the whole world."

"England, huh? I'd like to go there sometime."

"Art, you'd be amazed at all the places you'd travel to if you took up tennis. Why, you could go around the whole world playing in tournaments."

"England?"

"England, Australia, France, Italy, Spain, New York City—lots of places. Hey, maybe you could even make the Davis Cup team!"

Arthur stared blankly. "Davis Cup? What's that?"

"Well, every country has a team, and they play against one another to see who wins the world championship."

"And there are Negroes on our team?"

Charity's smile left his face. "No," he said softly. "There never have been. Not yet, anyway. But maybe you could be the first."

"Maybe *you* could," Art said. "They say you're one of the best black players in the country."

"That's what they say, huh?" Charity laughed. "Well, maybe I am. But I'm not *that* good."

"You're way better than me, anyway."

"Not for long," Charity said. "Not the way you're going—Champ."

Arthur continued to win, but he was running out of tournaments to compete in. There weren't that many for Negroes in Richmond.

One day Art talked his cousin Howard into going with him down to Byrd Park, in the

71

white neighborhood of Grant Park. Byrd Park had tennis courts, but Negroes weren't allowed to play on them.

"You sure it's okay to go down there?" Howard asked his cousin.

"Sure," Art said. "We'll just go over there and see what's going on. And we'll bring our rackets, just in case."

Arthur had been teaching Howard how to play tennis. Howard wasn't bad, but Art had to slow down a lot to play with him.

The two boys headed over to Byrd Park. When they got there, Art felt his usual courage drain right out of him. There wasn't another black face to be seen anywhere.

"Maybe we should go home, Arthur," Howard said, trying to drag him away.

"No, let's go on over to the courts," Art insisted. "I want to see them."

They started walking through the park. People stared at them—these two little Negro children who had the nerve to go where they weren't wanted. But no one tried to stop them.

"Just look like you know where you're going," Art told Howard. "Then they'll think we're just passing through."

The tennis courts were beautiful. They all had new nets, and there were even lights so that people could play at night. And there were so many courts! At Brookfield Park there were only four, and people were always waiting to use them. Here there were sixteen, most of them empty.

Arthur stood watching through the chain-link fence. He wished he could volley with these people and show them how well a black kid could play the "white man's game."

"You boys lost?"

Arthur and Howard gasped and turned around. Two big, tall white men were staring down at them, frowning.

"Uh, yeah," Arthur said. "We're . . . we're looking for Brookfield Park."

The two men laughed. "Boy, you *are* lost!"

They good-naturedly gave the boys directions back home. Art wondered if they would have been so friendly if they'd known the truth.

On their way back home Arthur said to Howard, "Someday I'm gonna play in a tournament there and win it."

"Huh?" Howard looked puzzled. "How are you gonna do that?"

"I don't know," Arthur said. "But I will. Just you wait and see."

School soon started up again. Arthur did well as usual. Things were good at home, too, even though Mrs. Berry made Arthur spend a lot of time with Johnnie, helping him with his homework.

"Nobody helped me with my homework when I was little," Art complained.

"Never you mind," said Mrs. Berry. "He needs your help, and he's your brother. That's all there is to it."

Art did as he was told, but he'd rather have been outside playing tennis.

One day in the spring, after his lessons had started up again, Ronald Charity sat him down for a talk.

"Arthur," he said, "you've really gotten to be a very good tennis player."

"Thanks!" Art said, a little surprised. Mr. Charity didn't usually hand out compliments like this.

"I'm sure you're going to win the Brookfield Park tournament again this summer."

"I mean to."

"But what then?"

"Huh?"

"I think you're running out of worlds to conquer here in Richmond."

Art thought of his and Howard's trip to Byrd Park. If only he could play against white kids as well as black, there'd be lots of challenges left for him.

"I also think," Charity went on, "that I've

taught you just about everything I can teach you. You need a new teacher now, Arthur—someone who can take you to the next level."

Art was shocked. "But I don't *want* a new teacher!" he said, leaping to his feet. "I want *you* to be my teacher!"

"Oh, I'll keep giving you lessons when you're here. But there's someone else I want you to learn from. He's a master teacher, and if he's willing to take you on as a student, I think he could turn you into a great player. He was Althea Gibson's coach, you know."

"He was?"

Art didn't know what to think. He was glad Mr. Charity thought he was that good. But he didn't want to take tennis lessons from a stranger. And what was that he'd said?

"What do you mean, when I'm here?"

"Dr. Johnson—that's the man's name—he runs a tennis academy out of his house in Lynchburg. You'd have to go there for two weeks over the summer and live with him and his family."

"No!" Art cried. "I don't want to go somewhere else to live!" He'd already done that—after his mother died—and he'd hated being away from home.

"Well, you think about it," Charity said. "Meanwhile, I've invited Dr. Johnson to watch you play at your next tournament. If he agrees to take you on, Arthur, I'd advise you to go. It's a great opportunity."

Arthur said he'd think about it. But he didn't like the idea of going away—even for two weeks.

Art won the tournament, with Dr. Johnson in the stands watching. Afterwards Charity introduced them.

"That was pretty impressive, young man," Dr. Johnson told him.

"Thanks," Art said, looking at the ground.

"But you need a lighter racket. That one's too big and heavy for you."

Art was surprised. This racket was a lot lighter than the first one he'd used.

"And you're throwing yourself at the ball too much—I think a lighter racket will help you with that, too. There are some other things as well. . . ."

He scratched his chin, then turned to Charity. "Well, Ronald, if this boy can get himself out to Lynchburg, I'll take him on. My son, Robert, and I will teach him—if his father approves, that is."

Arthur thanked Dr. Johnson. He knew he should feel lucky and grateful. In his heart, though, he hoped his father would say no.

Mr. Ashe wasn't keen about the idea at first. Arthur was not quite ten—younger than any of the other boys in Dr. Johnson's program. But after talking to Mrs. Berry and others, he decided it would be just the thing for Arthur. It would expand his horizons, and it would help him decide if he wanted his future to be about tennis. Mr. Ashe hoped that tennis would be Arthur's ticket to college and to the world beyond Richmond.

And so, that summer, Arthur found himself packing his suitcase for the long trip to Lynchburg, Virginia—more than a hundred miles away from home.

Lynchburg

Dr. Johnson's house was huge and grand. He was a medical doctor and had made quite a bit of money in his life. He now devoted his summers to helping young black tennis players improve their game. He wanted to teach them to be tennis champions, but even more important, he wanted them to be champions for their people.

The house was big enough to house two dozen boys. Some were from up north, and they were shocked to see that in Virginia blacks were still kept separate from whites.

Their reactions reminded Arthur of things he didn't like to think about, like how bad things were for Negroes. It just made him angry.

The boys' families did not have to pay for their time at Dr. Johnson's camp. Instead, to earn their keep, the boys helped out around the house.

They tended Dr. Johnson's gardens and flower beds, swept the floors, and cleaned the doghouse. Most of the boys didn't mind this at all—they were thrilled to have the chance to study tennis with a man like Dr. Johnson.

But not Arthur.

From the time he arrived, it was clear that life in Lynchburg would be nothing like his life in Richmond. There he played baseball, rode his bike, and swam in Brookfield Park's swimming pool. He played tennis only in the afternoons, and only if it wasn't too hot.

Here it was tennis, tennis, tennis all day long, and all evening, too. The boys woke at six thirty in the morning, went straight to the tennis courts behind the house, and started practicing. They worked on their game till breakfast, then again till lunchtime. After lunch it was time for exercising and work around the house. And after dinner there were movies—about tennis.

Or, if you didn't want to watch, there were shelves full of books to read—all about tennis.

Or, if you hadn't had enough tennis for one day, there was a ball hanging from a rope in the garage—you could go hit that for a while.

Arthur had never lived and breathed tennis twenty-four hours a day. The first few days at Dr. Johnson's were very hard for him.

The tennis lessons were a problem for him too. Over the past three summers Arthur had gotten used to Mr. Charity as his teacher. More than a teacher, Charity had also become a good friend.

Dr. Johnson was different—more like Arthur's dad. He was strict, and he demanded that the boys do everything his way.

Dr. Johnson's son, Robert, who did a lot of the teaching, was the same way. He wanted Arthur to change many things about the way he played—especially the way he held the racket.

"The way you grip it only works for people with strong wrists," he told Arthur, "not for skinny little wrists like yours. You should try this grip instead. . . ."

"I'm not changing my grip," Arthur told him flatly.

"What?"

"Mr. Charity taught me to hold it this way."

"Mr. Charity's not your teacher anymore. I'm your teacher now, and you'll do it my way."

"I won't," Arthur said stubbornly. "I like my grip—it's more comfortable."

The younger Mr. Johnson walked over to

his father. Arthur could hear them from across the court.

"That boy won't listen to a thing I tell him," he told Dr. Johnson. "Everything's a fight with him. I think we should send him back home."

"He's young still," Dr. Johnson replied. "We've never tried to teach a boy that young. I'd hate to give up on such a talented boy, Robert. This experience could mean so much to him. Let me try something else first."

"All right," his son said. "But if it doesn't work, I think we should send him home."

Arthur was shocked to hear that they might send him home in disgrace. How could he ever face Mr. Charity if he failed? How could he face his father?

He soon found out. Several hours later his father arrived and took Arthur aside to speak to him. "Son, I hear there have been some problems between you and your teachers."

"Yes, Dad." Arthur knew what was coming. He knew he had done wrong, and his father was about to tell him so.

"Son, Mr. Charity sent you here because he felt you had already learned everything he could teach you. He believes Dr. Johnson knows more about tennis than he does."

Art said nothing. He knew in his heart that his father was right. But he felt ashamed that his father had had to come all the way to Lynchburg because of his behavior.

"Now, do you want to stay here or come home with me?"

"Stay here," Art whispered, the tears welling up in his eyes.

"We all want you to give tennis your best shot, Arthur," his father said. "Mrs. Berry and I, Mr. Charity . . . we're just not sure if *you* want it too."

"I'm not sure either, Dad," Art said in a soft voice.

"Well, why don't you use the rest of your

time here to find out, son? Why don't you follow the Johnsons' program and give it everything you've got? That way you'll find out if a future in tennis is really for you."

By the time his father left for Richmond, Arthur had decided to do just that.

For the next week and a half he worked harder than he'd ever worked in his life. He did everything the Johnsons asked him to do—except change his grip. And after a few days the Johnsons had to agree that the grip wasn't hurting his game any.

During the second week of the tennis camp Dr. Johnson loaded the boys into his big old Buick Electra 225, and they went off to play in a pair of junior tournaments sponsored by the ATA, the tennis association for black players.

"Now, you boys listen to me," Dr. Johnson said as he drove. "If a ball is close to the line, you give the point to your opponent, every time. And if the referee calls a point against you, don't complain. Don't talk back. Don't argue."

It's not fair, Art thought. *Why should we have to keep quiet if we know we're right?*

But Dr. Johnson insisted that they make a good impression. That was more important than winning any match, he said. One day soon, he hoped, they'd be playing in USLTA junior tournaments—where all the other players would be white. Everyone would be looking at them and judging them for their manners as well as their skill. Dr. Johnson wanted them to be ready and to be fine representatives of black America.

Arthur won both of his first two tournaments in the under-twelve division. And he behaved like a gentleman, too—just as Dr. Johnson had asked.

By the time he returned to Richmond late that summer, Art's tennis game had improved by leaps and bounds. Nobody at Brookfield Park could beat him now. No one except

Ronald Charity, and even *he* had to work hard at it.

Everyone could see that one day soon young Arthur Ashe would be the best black tennis player in all of Richmond.

A World of Change

In 1954 the Supreme Court, the highest court in the United States, ruled that it was against the law to separate blacks from whites in schools. It was the beginning of the civil rights movement, which would soon produce Dr. Martin Luther King Jr. as its leader.

In the South there was anger among white people who didn't want any changes. They didn't want their children to go to school with black children. And now the Court was making them do it.

Some people reacted with violence.

Negroes were beaten up, and many were killed over the next few years. But change was coming to the South and to Richmond.

Arthur could feel it. Twice more he went to Byrd Park with his racket, hoping he would be allowed to play with whites. He was sent away both times, with a warning not to come back. Silently he swore he *would* come back. Someday he would play there—and he would win.

That year he played a lot of baseball on his grade-school team. He switched positions, from second base (like Jackie Robinson) to pitcher (Satchel Paige became his new hero). He dreamed of becoming a professional baseball player more than ever. It was a world that was fast opening to blacks—unlike tennis.

Still, as his eleventh birthday rolled around, he began to look forward to another trip to Lynchburg—and more tournaments.

This time he made the most of his stay. He

woke before anyone else to hit the hanging tennis ball in the garage and to use the automatic ball machine, which fired serve after serve at him. Even after everyone else was tired out at the end of the day, he was still at it. Late at night he read books and magazines about tennis.

Because he was small in size, the Johnsons taught him to concentrate on hitting the ball where he wanted it to go, more than on blasting it past his opponents. His job, they said, was to keep the ball in play until the other guy made a mistake. They taught him to have a strategy—to use his mind to beat an opponent.

That summer he and the Junior Development Team, as Dr. Johnson called his students, traveled to several more tournaments. Arthur won every one of them in the under-twelve division. The following year he did even better, winning the ATA's national under-fifteen championship.

That year Mr. Ashe got married again, and

the new Mrs. Ashe moved in with them. Arthur liked her very much. But her arrival meant that Mrs. Berry had to move into the boys' room with them. That made things awfully crowded, as far as Art was concerned, but there wasn't much he could do about it.

By the time Arthur entered junior high school, everyone knew about his exploits. He joined the tennis team right away and was its instant star. He ran track as well and even played some basketball.

He wanted to join the football team too, but his father said, "Absolutely not. You may be taller now, but you're still thin as a rail. You'd break every bone in your body."

"They'd never catch me to tackle me, Dad!" Arthur protested, but it was no use. Mr. Ashe refused to sign the permission slip. Arthur never did get to play organized football.

Baseball was still his favorite sport, and he excelled on his junior high school team as a pitcher. He was getting too old and too tall for Little League by then, so the school team was his only chance to play.

In the summers he kept returning to Dr. Johnson's, except that now, with his father's permission, he went for a full month every year. It gave him more chances to play tennis against the best black players his age, not only in Virginia, but in neighboring states. In 1957 he won the ATA's national fifteen-and-under title, and the next year he would win it again.

One day Dr. Johnson came to Arthur and the boy who shared a room with him, Bobby Davis. Bobby was from the North and could never get used to the way things were in the South between whites and blacks.

Dr. Johnson said, "Arthur, I've signed you up to play in a tournament in Florida this weekend."

"Just me?"

"Just you, for this time. It's a long way to

travel—very expensive to take all the boys. And besides . . . this is a USLTA junior tournament."

"You mean . . ."

"That's right. Most of the other boys will be white."

"Most?"

Dr. Johnson cleared his throat. "All except you, Arthur. Look, if that makes you uncomfortable, we can—"

"No, I want to go," Art said. He remembered the times he'd gone to Byrd Park in Richmond and not been allowed even to step onto the courts.

"I chose you to represent our program because you're the best player we have. I also know you'll behave like a gentleman—and that's going to be the most important thing. These white folks have never had a black player on their courts before. I want them to get a good impression."

"I understand," Art said.

"But what if there's trouble?" Bobby asked. "I've heard terrible stories of what happens to black folks in places like Florida."

"It won't be like that," Dr. Johnson assured the boys. "This time we've been invited." He nodded, smiling. "Yes, change is coming, even in the world of tennis. Slowly—way too slowly—but it's coming, all right. And we're going to be a part of it."

Arthur went down to Florida and played in the tournament. Everyone treated him well, even though he was the only black player in the event. No one yelled at him or said anything nasty to him.

He knew why, too—it was because he "knew his place." If he'd told them what he really thought about black-white relations, they wouldn't have been so friendly. He was sure of it.

After that Art and the rest of Dr. Johnson's Junior Development Team played in many more tournaments that had been for whites only. Most of the time they were the first black players ever to play there.

They went to New Jersey, Maryland, Michigan, and Washington, D.C. But they also went to southern states like North Carolina, Florida, and Texas. In the South the reception was not always friendly. One night Arthur and Bobby were asleep in their room at the YMCA, where they were staying while the tournament went on.

In the middle of the night the boys awoke to the sound of a fierce crash. Arthur flicked on the light and gasped in horror. There was a huge ax sticking right through their door!

Clearly someone didn't want them there, playing tennis with whites and butting their noses in where they didn't belong.

But the boys stayed and played and won. And they did it while showing their best manners to everyone.

Arthur soon won quite a few USLTA tournaments, as well as many more on the ATA circuit.

He was so good that the USLTA ranked him number five nationwide among fifteen-and-under players. People were saying he was the best black tennis prospect since Althea Gibson.

Sometimes Dr. Johnson took only Arthur with him, because long-distance travel was expensive and Arthur was the best of his students. At these tournaments there were players from all over the country. But Art was often the only black player there.

Arthur was shy, but he was smart, good natured, and always agreeable. The other boys liked him right away—but being friends with a Negro boy was not always so easy.

One night at a tournament in Charlottesville, Virginia, a group of the white players talked Art into going to the movies with them. Most of them were from northern states and didn't know what was coming.

Art knew, though. He warned them, but they refused to believe him.

They lined up outside the movie theater to

buy their tickets. But when Arthur got to the front of the line, the cashier refused to sell him a ticket. "We're all sold out," she said, frowning at him.

"But you just sold all of *them* tickets," Art said.

"You know what I'm talking about," the lady said. "Don't pretend you don't."

"Hey," one of Art's friends said to her, "if he can't go in, we're not going in either."

"Fine with me," said the woman. "I'll give you back your money."

And she did. The boys went home, some of them in tears. They were hurt and angry about what had happened.

Arthur was the one hurt most of all. But he didn't say anything. He was used to it from a lifetime of growing up in the South.

He could only hope that someday things would be different and that he himself would be a part of that change.

Growing Up Fast

Three years had passed since the Supreme Court declared that blacks and whites should go to the same schools. Things were changing all over America. But in the South, and especially in Richmond, they were changing slower than everywhere else.

Back when the law was passed, in 1954, Arthur and all his friends had talked about what it would be like, going to school with white kids. They were sure it would happen soon. But here it was, 1957, and not much had changed. White kids still went to separate schools. And most of Richmond's tennis courts—and tournaments—were still reserved for whites.

If things didn't change soon, Arthur would never be able to develop into a world-class tennis player because he would never get to play against the strongest competition.

Young as he was, Arthur was determined to try and change things. One day he told his cousin Howard, "I'm going to go over to Byrd Park again. That big department store down town is holding a junior tournament, and I'm going to try to get into it."

"Are you crazy, Arthur?" Howard said, his eyes widening in fear. "Do you know what they'll do to you over there?"

"I'm not afraid," Art said. It was a lie— inside he was terrified. But he wasn't going to let that stop him. "You just watch me."

"I'm not going over there!" Howard said, shaking his head.

"All right, then. I guess you'll read all about it in the papers tomorrow."

So that day Art went down to Byrd Park. Once or twice along the way he looked over his shoulder and caught a glimpse of Howard, hiding behind a tree. It made Art smile to think of his little cousin, too scared to come with him, but too curious to stay away.

There was a big crowd at Byrd Park's tennis courts. Many people looked at the young black boy with a tennis racket, but no one said anything to him. If he had come to watch, well, times were changing. As long as he didn't take up seats reserved for whites, they would not raise a fuss.

Still, he got a lot of dirty looks. Art saw them, but he just stood there quietly. He knew what was coming.

A week ago he'd talked Mr. Charity and his father into entering his name in the competition. Mr. Charity had agreed to be here, just in case there was any trouble.

Where was he, anyway? Art looked around, but he didn't see his coach and friend anywhere.

There was Howard, though, hiding behind a bush. Much good he'd be if there was a fight.

Art heard his name called by the tournament officials. "Arthur Ashe Jr."

"Here!" he said.

Everyone turned and looked at him. A terrible silence fell on the crowd.

The man in charge stepped up to him. "I'm sorry, son," he said. "You can't play in this tournament."

Art held his ground. "I have a right to play," he said. "This is America."

The man cleared his throat. "This is Richmond, son. And this tournament is closed to Negroes."

"I demand to play," Art said. He could feel his whole body shaking, but he didn't back away.

"Get that kid outta here!" someone

shouted. Someone else screamed curses at him, and others started yelling too, calling him bad names. A few even threatened to hurt him.

Art knew it was time to go. He took a deep breath and said, "I'm going, all right. But someday I'll be back. Someday you'll be sorry you treated me this way."

He walked away with his head held high. But inside he was like an angry volcano, about to erupt.

"Wow! Arthur, that was so brave!" Howard said as he caught up to his cousin. The younger boy was out of breath, and he looked terrified but proud.

"Was it?" Art asked, giving a little laugh. "Yeah, I guess it was, at that."

By the time he entered Maggie Walker High School, Arthur had grown much taller. He was still thin, but much stronger than the year before. He looked forward to joining the

baseball team, but that would have to wait a year. First-year students weren't allowed on the varsity squad.

In the meantime he ran track, played some basketball, and above all, played tennis. He joined the tennis team the very first week and proceeded to beat just about everyone he played against. One day that year he even beat his friend and former coach, Ronald Charity—the best black player in the state of Virginia!

Correction: The best black player in Virginia was now Arthur Ashe Jr.!

But that wasn't enough for him: he wanted to be more than the best *black* player—he wanted to be the best player *period*.

In his second year of high school Art finally joined the baseball team. All year long he had waited for this moment. Baseball was still his favorite sport, just as it always had been.

But being on the team was a disappointment. As a first-year relief pitcher, he almost never got to play. Game after game he sat on the bench and watched his teammates play, waiting for a chance to show what he could do.

Then one day his moment arrived. In the sixth inning of a game against a team from Petersburg, his coach signaled to him to warm up and come into the game.

The Richmond team was in trouble, but Art was ready. For weeks he'd imagined this moment. He tried to keep himself calm. He knew that if he got too excited, he wouldn't be able to throw the ball over the plate.

His first pitch was a fastball. The batter swung through it. "Strike one!" called the umpire.

The next pitch was a foul ball. With two strikes, Arthur threw the ball slower, surprising the batter. "Strike three, you're out!" called the umpire as the ball popped into the catcher's glove.

The next batter hit a weak ground ball for the second out. And the third batter struck out swinging. Arthur had pitched a perfect inning!

His team mobbed him in the dugout. Art had never been so happy in his entire life! But when it came time for the next inning, the coach called on someone else to pitch instead of him.

Arthur was stunned and angry. His friends on the team came over to him and told him they were shocked too. But nobody dared say anything to the coach.

After that game Arthur told himself he would spend every spare minute from then on practicing his pitching. Someday that coach would see how good he could really be. Someday he would show them all!

The next morning in homeroom his teacher told him the principal wanted to see him.

Arthur wondered why—he hadn't done anything bad, had he? He was a good student and never got into any trouble. What could the principal want with him?

"Sit down, Arthur, sit down," the principal said. "I understand you're very interested in baseball."

"Yes, sir."

"Well, I'll tell you what, Arthur. I'm sure you know you're one of the best tennis players anybody's ever seen around here."

Arthur wanted to smile, but something told him there was bad news coming.

He was right.

"I believe that if you concentrate on tennis, you could be one of the best players in the world someday," the principal said. "If you split your focus, if you try to be good at too many other things, you may never become the best you can be at tennis."

"But I like baseball bett—," Art started to say.

"So I am taking you off the baseball team. From here on in you'll be free to devote all your extra time to tennis. And I know you will make this school very proud."

"But—"

"That will be all, Arthur. You can go back to class now."

"Y-yes, sir."

That was the end of Arthur's school baseball career. He didn't like it, but there wasn't much he could do about it.

He complained to his father, but Mr. Ashe refused to get involved. "If your principal thinks that's what's best for you, Arthur, I have to agree. Think what would happen if you hurt yourself playing baseball."

There was no use arguing. Arthur had to accept it. Because he was so good at tennis, he would never get the chance to play professional baseball like Jackie Robinson.

He would have to find new heroes. Tennis heroes. And he did find one, in Pancho Gonzales.

Gonzales was the world champion of professional tennis. Art had first seen him play when he came to Richmond for an exhibition. After that he had watched Gonzales on TV whenever he could.

Gonzales was born in Mexico, although he grew up in Los Angeles. He was an outsider, like Arthur, in the white tennis world.

Art loved the way Pancho played the game. He was smooth and cool, just like Arthur tried to be. And if dark-skinned Pancho could break through to the top ranks of the "white man's game," so could he.

"You could be that good someday," Ronald Charity told him as they watched Gonzales on TV one day.

Art stared at the TV screen, at the amazing Pancho Gonzales. "That would be a dream come true," he said.

Charity smiled. "I'll tell you what, Arthur," he said. "In my opinion it's just a matter of time."

The World Beyond Richmond

Now that he played only tennis and no other sports, Arthur found that his schoolmates treated him differently. Before, everyone had wanted to be his friend. Now they all made fun of him.

When he'd played all those other sports, the ones everyone knew about, they'd admired him. But none of the kids at his high school cared about tennis. And because Arthur was also an A student and his teachers all loved him, the other kids were jealous.

Arthur had never been unpopular before.

Part of him wanted to give up tennis and stop trying so hard to get good grades, so that the other kids would like him better. But he knew that wouldn't be a good idea. He knew he had to think of his future. And in case he ever forgot, his dad, his stepmother, Mrs. Berry, Mr. Charity, and Dr. Johnson were all there to remind him.

All the while Arthur continued to improve at tennis. He was now over six feet tall, and although he was still skinny, he had grown very strong and powerful. His long arms helped him reach any ball hit to him, and his long legs enabled him to cover the entire court with speed and grace.

During his high school years he became just about unbeatable. Of course, this was just on the black high school circuit. In Virginia, in spite of the new laws, blacks and whites still did not mix on the tennis court.

That meant that Arthur never got a chance to see how well he could do against all other players. It also meant that his progress was slower than it should have been.

Every summer, for one month, Dr. Johnson took him to tournaments all over the U.S. In 1959 he won the ATA's national junior tournament. Even more amazing, he won their national men's tournament. That meant he was the best black player in the whole United States—and he was still only sixteen years old! Among all amateur players under eighteen, he was ranked forty-fourth that year. He was the highest-ranked black player in the nation.

In a way, though, it wasn't really fair. Most of those white boys got to play tennis year-round. Either they lived where it was warm in the winter, or they could play on indoor courts in the cold weather. But there were no indoor courts in Richmond open to black people. Arthur could play tennis only half the year.

He wondered how good he could be if, like

the white players, he could play tennis all year long.

Dr. Johnson wondered too. So did many other people who were watching Arthur's rapid progress. One of them was Richard Hudlin, who had once been the coach of the University of Chicago's tennis team.

Hudlin now lived in Saint Louis. He told his friend Harry Burris, the coach at Washington University, about Arthur's predicament— being stuck in Richmond, where he had no chance to improve his game any further.

Burris knew that Arthur wasn't old enough yet to go to college. But he was willing to bring Arthur to Saint Louis for his senior year in high school and pay for all his expenses. Hudlin offered to let Arthur stay with his family for the year and to be his coach during that time.

At first Arthur's father and stepmother weren't sure what to say. Art was still so young. It had been hard for Mr. Ashe to let his oldest son go for one month at a time to Dr. Johnson's. This would be for a whole year!

Still, it was a wonderful offer. In Missouri, Arthur would be able to play tennis all year long against some of the best young players in the country, black and white.

Besides, Mr. Ashe knew that Arthur was being made fun of at school here in Richmond—even though Arthur never complained about it.

Mr. Ashe spoke to Dr. Johnson and Mr. Charity, and all agreed that Arthur should go to Saint Louis. Everyone agreed—except Arthur himself.

He didn't want to go. Richmond was his home! He'd always lived there!

He remembered how hard his first summer at Dr. Johnson's had been. This was bound to be much worse, he thought. At Dr. Johnson's he'd worked on his tennis so hard, but only for a month! He was sure he couldn't keep up that pace all year long.

And who were these people he'd be stay-ing with? What if he didn't even like them? What if *they* didn't like *him*? What if *no one* there liked him?

In the end, though, he agreed to go. Everyone he knew, loved, and trusted was telling him it was best for him. No matter how he felt inside, he had to put his faith in them. And so in September 1960 he got on the bus for Saint Louis.

Except for short visits, he would never live in Richmond again. The wider world was now his home and would be for the rest of his life.

Saint Louis Blues

Life in Saint Louis didn't start out so well for Arthur. As he had feared, he didn't like living with the Hudlin family. They were very strict, just like Dr. Johnson and his own father. Except that here he didn't have any friends or family. He was all alone and very unhappy.

Why does everyone want me to give up everything for tennis? he wondered. He wished he could just take things easy—hang out with friends after school, go to movies, go out to parties and on dates with girls, sleep late on weekends if he wanted to.

But no—he had to work every spare moment on his tennis game. Between that and homework and early bedtimes, his first few weeks in Saint Louis were miserable.

He sometimes wished he were his little brother, Johnnie. Johnnie was growing big and strong and was a star at school in base-ball, track, swimming—even football. Art couldn't help being jealous when he thought about it.

Slowly, though, things started to get better for him. He did well in his classes right away. In Richmond that would have made him unpopular, but not here.

It turned out that everyone already knew all about him—he was the future star of the school's tennis team, brought all the way from Virginia to give them a championship. Girls paid attention to him, and once he started winning tennis matches, everyone wanted to be his friend.

He was still shy, of course. Nothing had

changed that. And the Hudlins were very strict about his hours. So he didn't go out partying or dating much. After a while he resigned himself to it. He had come here to work on his tennis. That was what his father, Dr. Johnson, and Mr. Charity all wanted him to do.

As the weather grew colder, he found himself practicing tennis indoors, as much as five hours every day. Mr. Hudlin worked with him to change his game.

Arthur had been taught by Mr. Charity and the Johnsons to be a baseline player, hanging back at the line and waiting for the ball to get to him, then hitting it back accurately, just where he wanted it, and hoping the other player made a mistake.

"That was fine when you were small and weak," Mr. Hudlin told him. "But now you're a big, strong guy, even if you are a little thin. I want you to attack the net—rush up there and hit the ball back before the other guy can position himself. Just slam it back as hard as you can, then rush the net. And shorten your backswing—you'll get to the ball quicker that way."

That type of play was called serve and volley. It meant you had to hit the ball before it bounced or just as it was rising from its bounce. It meant you had to be fast and very strong. And so Arthur worked on his speed and strength as well as his tennis.

Soon his efforts began to pay off. In November of that year, 1960, he entered the USLTA's National Junior Indoor Tennis Championship. It had always been Dr. Johnson's dream for one of his Junior Development Team members to win a major tournament of the formerly all-white USLTA.

Arthur made it to the final round and found himself facing nineteen-year old Frank Froehling, the top-ranked player in the tournament. It took four hours and five sets, but Arthur won the match.

It was the first time an African American had won a major USLTA tournament. It meant that Arthur was now the best tennis player under nineteen years of age in the whole country (at least on indoor courts)—black or white. The entire tennis world took notice of the stunning news.

It was the biggest thrill of his life so far. At that moment he felt all his hard work had been worth it. And that victory was just the start of greater things to come.

The following month he went home for Christmas vacation. On the night he arrived, the telephone rang.

"It's for you, Arthur," said his father.

Arthur picked up the phone. "Hello?"

"Arthur? This is J. D. Morgan—I'm the coach of the tennis team at UCLA."

Arthur knew that UCLA was the University of California at Los Angeles—home of the top college tennis team in the country.

"Yes, sir?"

"You know, I've been following your career since you were fifteen," Mr. Morgan said.

"You have?"

"Yes, and I've spoken to Dr. Johnson about you a few times too."

"Really? He never said anything to me."

"Well, I guess he didn't want to disappoint you, in case things didn't work out."

"I . . . don't understand," Arthur said.

"Well, Arthur, I'd like you to come west in September and attend our university. There's a place on our tennis team just waiting for you. And you'll have a full scholarship—the first we've ever offered to a black tennis player—so your family won't have to come up with any money. How does that sound to you?"

Arthur was stunned and amazed. He couldn't believe his ears! Sure, UCLA was thousands of miles away from home, in California, but so what? He was already in Saint Louis, almost halfway there.

"It sounds fantastic!" he said.

"Now, I know you're going to be hearing from a lot of other schools. They're all going to want you on their tennis team. But I hope you'll decide to join us."

"Are you kidding?" Art said. There was no question in his mind—this was the chance he'd always dreamed of. At UCLA, he'd be on a team that featured some of the best young players in the world. "Count me in!"

"Well, that's great!" Mr. Morgan said. "We'll see you in September, then?"

"Don't worry," said Arthur, "nothing could keep me away!"

The next few months were a happy blur for Arthur. That spring he reached the semifinals of the National Jaycees and National Juniors tournaments, and he won the National Interscholastic event as well.

By the time he graduated—with the highest grade point average in his class—he was ranked the number five junior player in America (black or white) and was a member of the honorary Junior Davis Cup team.

Arthur remembered Mr. Charity telling him about the Davis Cup, where you played for your country against teams from other nations. Someday, he hoped, he would be on the real Davis Cup team.

He would get his chance—and sooner than he would have thought possible.

College Days

When Arthur first left Richmond for Dr. Johnson's summer tennis camp, he had been scared and unhappy. He'd felt even worse about going away for a year to Saint Louis. But now things were different.

Going west to Los Angeles in the fall of 1961, eighteen-year-old Arthur Ashe was happy and excited. He knew UCLA was a wonderful school with a great tennis program. He also knew that this was his ticket to the wider world.

Over the past few years his tennis game

had gotten better and better. He had been a star on the ATA circuit and a star in Saint Louis and was now a star on the USLTA Junior Circuit. He fully expected to be a star at UCLA, too.

He was in for a surprise.

When he arrived, he found that he was ranked at number three on the team, behind his roommate, Charles Pasarell (number one), the national junior champion, and Dave Reed (number two), the Southern California junior champion. The team across town at the University of Southern California (USC) featured Dennis Ralston, the number one college player in the country.

The competition at the college level was much tougher than Arthur was used to. The players were better, stronger, and faster, and the whole game was quicker and more intense. It took some time for Arthur to get used to the fact that here he was just another player on a very good team.

There were many things he loved right away about being in Southern California. For one thing, the weather was fine and you could play outdoors all year-round.

For another thing, his hero, Pancho Gonzales, lived nearby. Arthur soon made friends with Pancho and began practicing with him regularly. These sessions, with the experienced professional giving him pointers, did wonders for Arthur's game.

Another thing he loved about UCLA was that, for the first time, nobody was looking over his shoulder. Until then his father, Mrs. Berry, Mr. Charity, Dr. Johnson, and Mr. Hudlin had all watched over him day and night, making sure he didn't stay out too late at parties or spend too much time with friends or dates.

Here he was on his own, at least socially. He began dating girls more often and spending more time with friends.

One of his best friends was Charles

Pasarell, his roommate. Born in Puerto Rico, Pasarell was also a kind of tennis outsider, although unlike Arthur and Pancho Gonzales, he didn't have very dark skin, so it was easier for him to avoid unwanted attention at tennis tournaments.

Arthur was still something rare—a black tennis player at the highest levels of the game. He now moved in a tennis world where the clothes were as white as the spectators and the players. And in that world he would always stand out.

Art knew it and accepted it, although it sometimes made him angry. He learned to use it to his advantage, realizing that he was a big drawing card, bringing crowds to tournaments to see him play. Someday, he thought, he might even make money as a tennis professional.

His coach, J. D. Morgan, was the toughest one Arthur had ever had. Art thought he was a great teacher, and tried extra hard to please him. Still, it wasn't like he was playing *for* his

129

coach, the way he had played for Mr. Charity and Dr. Johnson and Mr. Hudlin. Now he was playing for his team—and for himself.

Tennis had become more to him than just a game. He was beginning to think of it as his future.

Besides tennis, classes, and fun, Arthur also had to work 250 hours each year to earn his scholarship money. Among other things, he had to keep the courts clean and tidy, but he didn't mind. It just gave him more time to be around tennis.

During his second year in college—1962—Arthur's hard work began to pay off. He beat Dave Reed, his teammate, and moved up to UCLA's number two spot, behind Pasarell. He also won the Southern California Sectional Championships, which came with an automatic invitation to play at Wimbledon the following June.

Wimbledon! Arthur remembered Mr. Charity telling him about it. The oldest, most important tournament in the world—and he was going to play in it!

But first there was the National Collegiate Athletic Association (NCAA) championship to play in. The two teams in the finals were UCLA and its crosstown rival, the USC. Arthur played well enough to make it to the semifinals, where he lost to the man who wound up winning the championship, Dennis Ralston.

Arthur was disappointed, but he had other things to think about. He soon got on an airplane and flew to a foreign country for the first time in his life.

England amazed him—cars driving on the wrong side of the road, double-decker buses, everybody speaking with a strange accent, but most of all, Wimbledon itself. The classic old tennis club on the outskirts of London was like tennis heaven. The lawns were the greenest he'd ever seen, and everyone spoke in whispers, as if it were a holy place.

At first he felt a little lost in England. Arthur was, as usual, the only black in the tournament, and here none of his friends were with him.

He would be playing against the greatest amateur players in the world—with thirty thousand white people in white clothing watching his every move.

In his first two matches Arthur impressed the crowds by defeating his opponents with flair, grace, style, and power.

In the third round he faced America's number one player, Chuck McKinley. Arthur had faced him before, when UCLA played McKinley's school, Trinity University. McKinley beat Arthur three sets to none and went on to win the tournament.

Arthur didn't feel too bad about it, though. He had played well in his first Wimbledon, and he felt sure there would be many more. Someday, he promised himself, he would make it all the way to the finals—and maybe even win tennis's greatest trophy.

After Wimbledon, Arthur flew to Budapest, Hungary, for another European tournament. There he made it all the way to the semifinals before losing in five sets to Denmark's Torben Ulrich.

By the time he returned home, he had jumped in the U.S. amateur tennis rankings from twenty-eighth, when he'd entered UCLA, all the way to sixth.

Along the way his game had changed, from one that depended on outlasting his opponent to a style featuring sheer power and blinding serves. That made him a much more dangerous player on faster surfaces, like hard courts and grass, than on clay, a softer surface where his old, slower baseline style worked better.

That summer he won the U.S. Hard Court Championships in Chicago—a victory that landed him an invitation to play on the U.S. Davis Cup team, along with Dennis Ralston, Chuck McKinley, and Marty Riessen.

It had been one of Arthur's lifelong dreams, and now it was coming true. He was the first black ever to play on the U.S. team. Even better, the coach that year was none other than his hero and friend, Pancho Gonzales!

In his first Davis Cup match, against Venezuela, Arthur defeated his opponent in just three sets, losing only two games along the way. He would have liked to stay on and play in more matches for his country, but he had to get back to UCLA in time for the fall semester.

By now his friend Charlie Pasarell had graduated, and Arthur was UCLA's number one player. He and USC's Dennis Ralston traded victories all through the year.

In 1964 Congress passed the Civil Rights Act, making blacks and whites officially equal in all things. Keeping the races separate was now against federal law.

Things were starting to change quickly,

even in the South. The year before, Dr. Martin Luther King Jr. had given his famous "I Have a Dream" speech. On UCLA's campus Arthur, who was now a celebrity, was urged by other black students to take a stand on civil rights.

Part of him wanted to stand up and speak his mind, but he felt that it wasn't time for that yet. First he had to become one of the best, most famous tennis players in the world. Then whatever he said would get more attention. For now he had to concentrate on his tennis.

That June he was back at Wimbledon. This time he made it all the way to the fourth round before losing to the eventual champion, Roy Emerson of Australia.

After Wimbledon he continued to play well on grass courts, reaching the finals of the Pennsylvania Grass Court Championships before losing to McKinley.

Next up were the Eastern Grass Court

Championships in New Jersey. This time Arthur went the distance, winning his first major championship on grass. Along the way he beat Dennis Ralston in three straight sets; Gene Scott, again in three sets; and Clark Graebner in the finals.

That victory earned Arthur an invitation to play that September in the U.S. National Championships at Forest Hills in New York. There he won his first three matches, before losing in the quarterfinals to Tony Roche of Australia. It was a good first showing at Forest Hills, but it was only the start of big things to come.

That fall Arthur also won another major prize—this one for his behavior off the court. In the gentleman's game of tennis Arthur Ashe Jr. was presented with the Johnston Award for sportsmanship.

It was a great honor, but more than that, it showed the world that blacks could be more than janitors and servants—they could be champions, and they could do it with manners every bit as polished as those of whites.

By the end of that year Arthur was ranked number three amateur tennis player in the United States, behind only Ralston and McKinley.

In 1965 he did even better, winning the NCAA singles title *and* doubles title (with Ian Crookenden). He also won all four of his Davis Cup matches, made it to the fourth round at Wimbledon, and made it to the semifinals at the U.S. championships in September.

At the end of that year he decided to travel to Australia and New Zealand for a series of tournaments and exhibitions. This meant that it would take him an extra semester to graduate, but Arthur felt it would be worth his while to get the experience of doing nothing but playing tennis for three straight months, ending with the Australian championships.

He wound up dazzling the folks down under by winning four of seven tournaments, coming in second in two others, and beating Emerson twice.

He then returned to UCLA, to finish his education. During this time, he achieved one more honor, and for Arthur, it was perhaps his most amazing achievement so far.

On February 4, 1966, the city of Richmond, Virginia, declared the day to be Arthur Ashe Day, honoring its most famous black citizen. Arthur was put up in the city's fanciest hotel—a place he wouldn't have been allowed to stay in just a couple of years before. He was entertained at a banquet in his honor and given a copy of the mayor's proclamation.

At the ceremony the mayor said, "This city is known around the world for many products— cigarettes, statesmen, and now Arthur Ashe, who has carried his country's banner around the world with dignity, honor, and skill."

To Arthur, it all seemed like a dream. There were his father, Dr. Johnson, and Mr. Charity, all saying wonderful things about him. Here he was in Richmond, living a moment he could never have imagined.

When it was his turn to speak, he said, "Ten years ago this would not have happened. It is as much of a tribute to Richmond and the state of Virginia as it is to me."

Arthur, now ranked the number two amateur in the country, graduated from UCLA that June. Everyone wondered whether he would soon be number one. But they had forgotten about one thing.

In order for Arthur to get his scholarship, he had had to join the ROTC program at school. ROTC paid for schooling in exchange for serving three years in the armed forces upon graduation.

It was now time for Arthur Ashe to serve his country. Immediately upon graduating, he joined the U.S. Army as a second lieutenant, reporting for duty at Fort Lewis, Washington. For the next three years he would be known as Lieutenant Ashe.

During the first two years of his service he served as a tennis instructor at the U.S. Military Academy at West Point, New York. That allowed him to perfect his game, but it wasn't the same as playing in world-class tournaments. Arthur played in very few of those in 1966 and 1967, and he didn't do very well. He did play in the Davis Cup, though, winning his first nine matches before suffering a pair of defeats.

Still, tennis fans started to forget about Arthur Ashe. To them, he was a piece of history that had now faded away with time.

Then came 1968.

Arthur Ashe, Champion

The year 1968 was an important one in world history. Everywhere society was in turmoil. America's war in Vietnam was going badly, with many soldiers dead and injured. At home antiwar protests reached a peak.

Then, in April, Dr. Martin Luther King Jr. was assassinated by a white man in Memphis, Tennessee. Despite Dr. King's lifelong devotion to nonviolent protest, black neighborhoods all over the country erupted in violent riots, fueled by anger over his murder.

At the Olympics that summer black

American athletes receiving their medals raised fists in protest when "The Star-Spangled Banner" was played.

In the Middle East terrorism reared its ugly head. In Europe, too, there were riots and bombings. The world seemed on the verge of revolution.

In the tennis world too things were changing. Until that year tennis professionals—the best players in the world—had not been allowed to play in any of the world's most prestigious tournaments. Wimbledon and the Australian, French, and U.S. championships—even the Davis Cup, tennis's version of the Olympics—were closed to them.

But in 1968 all that changed with one bold ruling by the International Tennis Federation (ITF). From that time on, professionals and amateurs would be able to compete against one another in major tournaments.

It was a huge step forward for tennis, and

as a result the sport would soon become much more popular worldwide.

For Arthur, though, the changes made things more difficult.

Now, in his last year of service, he would be allowed more freedom to travel abroad for tournaments. But to win them, he would have to beat not only the best amateurs in the game, but the best players *period*. It was a much tougher task than he'd ever imagined it would be.

While at West Point he had continued to perfect his strokes. In addition to his cannon-ball serve, he now featured a devastating backhand with topspin. Thanks to the army's tough workouts, he had also improved his flexibility, endurance, and strength, as well as his mental approach to the game.

Twenty-four years old and at the peak of his physical powers, he was ready for the challenge.

The most incredible tennis year in Arthur's

life began with a dream come true. It ended with another.

In March he returned to Richmond. He had gone home to visit several times in the past few years, but this time was different. He was there as a member of the U.S. Davis Cup team, for a match at Byrd Park—the very place where he'd been banished years before.

When he went onto the court, he saluted his father, Mr. Charity, and Dr. Johnson. Arthur's brother, Johnnie, had joined the Marine Corps and could not be there, but Cousin Howard, now all grown up, was there to watch the great event. The last time he'd hidden behind a bush. Now he was sitting in the front row, waving and cheering.

Arthur looked around at the stands. In the old days, just a few years ago, only whites could sit there. Now his friends and family were everywhere.

How things had changed!

That week Arthur easily defeated all six of his opponents, from three different countries. He played with an inner fire he had rarely shown before. Everyone gasped at the brilliant shots he made. Newspaper reporters took notice too. Soon the whole sports world was buzzing about Arthur Ashe's return to the top ranks of tennis.

June came, and Arthur arrived at Wimbledon filled with purpose. This year, for the first time, the best players in the world—professionals like John Newcombe, Ken Rosewall, his old friend and mentor Pancho Gonzales, and Rod Laver, the number-one player in the world—would be playing in the tournament.

Arthur was glad about the change. He had decided that if he was going to win, why not do it by beating the best?

That kind of confidence helps any player do his best, and Arthur won his first three matches without losing a single set.

In the fourth round he faced John Newcombe, who had won both Wimbledon and the U.S. nationals the year before as an amateur. Now he was a professional who could devote all his time to tennis. Arthur, an amateur, could practice only part-time. That made him a distinct underdog. Newcombe was seeded (ranked) fourth in the tournament, while Arthur was only thirteenth.

Nevertheless, Arthur won the first two sets, 6–4, 6–4. The crowd buzzed with excitement, smelling a major upset. Newcombe rallied in the third set, winning 6–1, and he won the fourth set too, 6–4.

The crowd held its breath for the fifth and final set. Arthur focused on breaking his opponent's serve. In the eighth game of the set he finally succeeded, putting a backhand smash past Newcombe's outstretched racket. Arthur served out the next game, and the match was his!

In the quarterfinals he faced Tom Okker,

the "Flying Dutchman." Arthur outlasted him in five grueling sets and made it into the semifinals.

Also making it in was Clark Graebner, a friend and Davis Cup teammate of Art's. The two friends could not believe their good fortune. In the first Wimbledon of the Open Era they had excelled. Perhaps they would meet in the finals!

For now Art's opponent was none other than the world's number one player, Rod Laver of Australia, a left-handed powerhouse playing at the top of his game. Laver proved to be too much for Arthur, defeating him easily. The great run was over, at least for the moment.

But Arthur did not feel defeated. In fact, just the opposite.

He played only part-time, yet he had been one of the last four men standing in a major open tournament.

From now on, with the army paying his

salary but demanding little of him, he would be able to practice full-time. He may not have won Wimbledon that year, but he could tell that his best tennis was yet to come.

After a loss at the U.S. Clay Court Championships in July, Arthur would not lose another match for more than two months. In that time he ran off an incredible string of twenty-six straight singles victories.

In August, in the middle of the streak and one week after helping defeat Spain in a Davis Cup match, he arrived at the U.S. Amateur Championship in Massachusetts. It was a tournament he had always dreamed of winning.

He was entered in both the singles and doubles competitions. Coming off so many matches in a row, he felt exhausted. His doubles team was soon eliminated, which turned out to be a good thing. For the rest of the singles tournament Arthur was strong enough to defeat every opponent he faced.

In the finals he found himself facing his Davis Cup teammate Bob Lutz. The temperature was ninety degrees, and after an hour or so the heat began to catch up with Arthur. He lost a long, exhausting third set and found himself down two sets to one.

Most players go off to the locker room between sets, to cool off and change shirts. Lutz now did just that. But Arthur stayed behind. He wanted to get right back on the court. He did not want to lose his edge, his laser focus.

People in the stands wondered what he was up to. As soon as Lutz returned, Art bounded out onto the court, ready to play.

Right away everyone could see that something had changed. Arthur was unstoppable. He served ace after ace. He landed every shot exactly where he wanted to. He played with a fury that Lutz couldn't match.

Arthur won the fourth set, 6–0, and went on to win the fifth set too, 6–4.

The U.S. amateur crown was his!

For the first time a black man was ranked the number one amateur tennis player in America!

Soon, Arthur promised himself, he would be number one—amateur *or* professional.

The very next week, at Forest Hills, the first U.S. Open began. Arthur breezed through his first two matches and into the third round. There his opponent was none other than Roy Emerson.

Arthur had a long history with the Australian, who had recently turned professional. Arthur had notched his share of victories, but Emerson had beaten him in the Australian championship finals two years in a row.

It was time for payback.

Arthur beat Emerson in straight sets—6–4, 9–7, 6–3—to advance to the quarter-finals. In doing so, he played one of the best matches of his life; but mostly, nobody noticed. For on that same day Cliff Drysdale of South Africa had pulled off one of the biggest upsets of the year by beating the great Rod Laver.

It was a lucky break for Arthur. At least, that was the way his friend Clark Graebner saw it. "Laver is a tough opponent for anyone, and his game is particularly tough on you, Arthur," Graebner told him over dinner the night before the match.

He was right. Over their lifetimes Laver would compile a 22–3 record against Arthur Ashe, the only player in the world with that kind of record against him.

Art knew he was lucky. But that didn't mean that Drysdale was a pushover. After all, he had just beaten the number one player on the planet.

As Arthur and Clark ate their dinner that night, Art thought about Cliff Drysdale. He was a white man from South Africa, a country where blacks, who were a vast majority of the people, still suffered terribly at the hands of whites. The leader of the black opposition, a hero named Nelson Mandela, was imprisoned on an island fortress.

That day there had been calls from some black leaders for Arthur to refuse to play Drysdale, in protest of South Africa's racist policies.

Arthur knew that Drysdale didn't believe in his country's awful laws. He also felt that it would be better to play Drysdale and whup him than to stay away in protest. Besides, he was still in the army, and his actions would reflect on America's armed forces. He decided to play the match.

His decision angered many—but not for long. The following day Arthur stepped onto center court in Forest Hills and struck a blow for freedom by beating Drysdale in four grueling, magnificent sets of tennis.

In spite of his victory, some black activists thought he had made the wrong decision.

They continued to criticize Arthur for his quiet, peaceful way of doing things. But for Arthur the best way to show the way was to play great tennis and be a good citizen.

His opponent in the semifinals was none other than Clark Graebner. Neither friend really wanted the other to lose, but they both wanted very much to win. After losing the first set, Arthur came back to win the next three sets and the match. He was in the finals!

At that moment Arthur Ashe stood on the verge of his first grand slam event title. The grand slam comprises the four biggest events in tennis: the French Open, the Australian Open, the U.S. Open, and Wimbledon. To win one of them would be the achievement of a lifetime, something few players ever achieve.

His moment was now. His opponent: the Flying Dutchman, Tom Okker.

The first set seemed to last forever. Arthur

finally won, 14–12, but Okker didn't surrender. He roared back to take the second set, 7–5.

Arthur rallied to take the third set, 6–3, then Okker returned the favor in the fourth set. That set up a final and decisive fifth set.

The huge crowd cheered wildly, then fell silent. On the court it was scorching hot, and both players were close to exhaustion. The winner would be whichever man outlasted the other.

Arthur's feet hurt. His right hand was aching, and the racket felt as heavy as a shovel. His head was pounding and his eyes were burning from the glare of the sun. But he was in such superb physical condition from his army training that he was able to overcome it all.

In the set's second game Arthur broke Okker's service to take a 2–0 lead. The rest of the way he held his own, winning the games where he served, losing the ones where he didn't. In the end the score was 6–4.

Arthur Ashe Jr. was the champion of the very first U.S. Open tournament! It was the first major tournament in America where professionals and amateurs had competed with one another—and an amateur had won.

The crowd stood and gave him a thunderous ovation as Arthur wandered around in circles, his hands thrust upward in disbelief and delight. Then he took the trophy and lifted it high over his head.

He was the first black man in history to win a grand slam tennis event. Like the great Althea Gibson, he had broken the color barrier in tennis.

His father ran down from the stands to embrace him. "Well done, son!" he said. "Well done!"

Back at West Point they gave him another standing ovation. But Arthur's year was not yet done. "It's nice to hear the announcer say, 'Point, Ashe,'" he told the newspaper

reporters. "But I'd rather hear him say, 'Point, United States.'"

It was time for the Davis Cup. That fall Arthur, Graebner, Lutz, and Stan Smith combined to beat India and Australia to win the cup for their country.

That December, Arthur was given the year-end ranking of number one tennis player in America, amateur or professional.

It was a dream ending to a dream year. He had made it all the way to the top of the American tennis world.

In February he would be released from the army. Already he had received fabulous offers to turn professional. Soon he could be making as much as $100,000 a year.

His whole future lay ahead of him, looking very bright indeed.

Struggles

Arthur and the other Davis Cup team members followed up their victory in Australia with a tour of Southeast Asia at the beginning of 1969, covering nine countries—including Vietnam, where American troops were at war. They performed tennis exhibitions for military bases in several countries and were greeted like heroes everywhere they went.

When they got back to the United States, they were honored with a reception at the White House, where President Lyndon B. Johnson greeted them and shook their hands.

Arthur was treated like the biggest hero of all. Not only was he number one in America, but he was the best—and just about the only— major black player in the game.

All across the country young black boys took up tennis rackets and started to learn the game. "I want to be like Arthur Ashe!" they would say, just as Arthur had once said, "I want to be like Jackie Robinson!"

Following his discharge from the army, Arthur did not go back to Richmond to live. Instead he got himself a swank apartment in New York City.

"I am a citizen of the world," he said. He wanted to represent the hopes and dreams of all people everywhere, especially blacks.

In New York, Arthur was the toast of the town. His picture was on the cover of *Sports Illustrated* and *Life* magazines, and the *New Yorker* magazine did a long story about him. He was invited to every exclusive party and dated many beautiful, famous women—

including Diana Ross and supermodel Beverly Johnson. He did commercials for Coca-Cola, American Express, Head tennis rackets, and Catalina tennis wear. Money was pouring in. Arthur would soon be a wealthy man.

With all these distractions, and with a sore elbow to go with them, Arthur's tennis suffered somewhat in 1969. No one could expect to repeat such a year as he had had in 1968, when he had ten tournament victories. And he didn't—in 1969 he won only two tournaments.

But there was some consolation. He made it to the Wimbledon semifinals for the second year in a row, beating Pancho Gonzales along the way, but finally losing to Rod Laver, who won for the second year in a row. Then, in September, he helped his Davis Cup team win their second straight cup.

Off the court he was still being criticized by many blacks for his lack of commitment to the struggle for civil rights. Black communities in the U.S. were still in turmoil after the riots of the year before, and many leaders felt that Arthur should take more public stands in protest.

Arthur resisted, however. He was not a public person, in spite of his newfound fame. He preferred to fight his battles behind the scenes.

During the previous year's U.S. Open, Arthur had gotten to know South Africa's Cliff Drysdale. Since then Drysdale had left his native country, as a protest against its racist laws, to come live in the U.S.

He and Arthur had frequent conversations about life for blacks in South Africa, and Arthur decided he wanted to do something about it.

"I want to be the first black to play in the South African Open," he told his friend.

"Good luck," Drysdale told him. "They'll never let you in."

162

But Arthur was determined to try anyway. In 1969 he applied to South Africa for a visa so he could go and play in the tournament. His request was refused.

Arthur, however, did not take it lying down. He went to the USLTA and to the U.S. secretary of state. Supporters from around the world backed his cause and did a very good job of embarrassing South Africa in the press and on television.

Still the South Africans refused to let Arthur in. So Arthur struck back. He worked to get South Africa banned from Davis Cup play for its racist policies. In 1970 that country was expelled from the competition.

Seeing that Arthur had become a nonviolent leader of blacks, the U.S. government decided to send him in 1970, along with Stan Smith, to Africa as goodwill ambassadors. Smith was now the country's number one player, having passed Ashe the previous year.

The two players traveled together all over

Africa, stopping in Kenya, Nigeria, Tanzania, and Uganda. The following year Arthur returned to the continent of his ancestors, this time with Tom Okker, Charles Pasarell, and Marty Riessen, visiting many countries and inspiring children and adults alike wherever he went.

In Cameroon that year he saw an eleven-year old boy play and was very impressed with his talent. He arranged for the boy to be sent to France to study tennis. That boy was Yannick Noah, who at the age of twenty would win the French Open championship and become France's number one player.

Arthur was active in those years on another front as well. In allowing professionals and amateurs to play against one another, tennis had become a much more popular sport. All its major tournaments were now shown on TV, and there was lots of money from advertisers to go around.

But the players themselves were still

competing for small cash prizes. Arthur led an effort by the players to form their own union, to fight for their fair share of the profits their talent was bringing in.

In 1970 a tennis players' union was born. Arthur, one of the most respected players in the game, was elected treasurer and served in that job for several years. Because of the union top tennis players were soon playing for much bigger prizes.

In 1970 Arthur shook off all the distractions and, with his sore elbow healed, began to play his best tennis once again. He won the Australian Open that year, his second grand slam event title. By the time the year ended, he had won ninety-one matches, while losing only twenty. He captured eleven tournament titles and reached the finals in three others. It was almost as good a year for him as 1968.

The years 1971 through 1974, however, were not as good. In 1973 he turned thirty, the age at which most tennis players' careers start to decline.

True, there were many players Arthur's age and older who were still playing well—Rod Laver, Ken Rosewall, John Newcombe, and Tony Roche, among others. But a new crop of superteens had come along to challenge the veterans—players like Guillermo Vilas, Björn Borg, and Jimmy Connors (also known as the Brash Basher).

It wasn't so much that Arthur's game had faded; he did win eleven tournaments in those years, taking 70 percent of his matches in 1972 and 1973, and 76 percent in 1974. But other players were lifting their games, and the young tigers were knocking at the door.

Then there were Arthur's off-the-court activities. Newspapers began to suggest that his game was suffering—not only because of several minor injuries, but also because of all the distractions in his life. There was his work for the players' union and all his commercial contracts.

Arthur did want to focus more on his tennis. But something else happened in 1973 to grab his attention and energy. Finally the government of South Africa relented and allowed Arthur to get a visa for its national open.

Many black leaders were angry at Arthur for his decision to play. They felt he should not go. According to them, the only way to deal with South Africa was to boycott it—to shun it, as most of the world was doing by then.

Arthur insisted on going. After four years of knocking on the door, he was not about to turn away now. He knew it would be important for South African blacks to see him face-to-face—to sit in the stands and watch him play. But he had no idea just how important his visit would turn out to be.

With the boycott against it in full swing, the government of South Africa had become anxious to have athletes of any color come and compete there. To have a black athlete come was an even bigger success. The government felt that Arthur's decision to play would take some of the pressure off them to change their racist system.

Arthur was not a radical, but he knew he was in a good bargaining position. He demanded three things from the South African government before he would play there. He would not play before an all-white crowd, or one where blacks and whites were seated separately. He refused to accept the government's gesture of making him an "honorary white," and he demanded to be allowed to go anywhere in the country he wanted to go.

South Africa agreed to all his requests. In November of 1973 Arthur, together with his agent and his coach, flew across the Atlantic. When he entered Ellis Park Stadium for his first match, Arthur was cheered by a sellout crowd of whites and blacks. Until that day no black fans had been allowed inside. Arthur's strong stand had made the difference.

Arthur won his first match in straight sets, to the great delight of the crowd. In the following days he kept on winning, not losing a single set until he reached the finals. There he lost in straight sets to the new king of men's tennis, young Jimmy Connors.

Arthur also played doubles in the South African Open, teaming up with Tom Okker, "the Flying Dutchman." The pair won the doubles title. To Arthur, it was one of the most important victories of his life. From that day on, and for all time, the name of a black player would be displayed on the list of South African Open tennis champions.

While he was in South Africa, Arthur took the opportunity to visit the places where blacks lived. These places were called townships. But they were really gigantic slums where people of color lived in poverty and misery, while their white neighbors, only a few miles away, lived lives of comfort, even luxury.

The people of Soweto, South Africa's largest township, welcomed Arthur with open arms, like a conquering hero. To them, he was inspiring—the vision of a free black man, walking the earth with his head held high, successful even in the world of whites. He played tennis with grace, elegance, style, and power. He spoke to whites as their equal and expressed himself with intelligence and wisdom.

Most South African black leaders were in prison, like the great Nelson Mandela, who had been locked up in an island fortress for nine years by then. But the people of Soweto could look at Arthur and see a future of freedom for themselves.

For Arthur it was an emotional visit. The people here lived in such terrible conditions—much worse than those of blacks in the U.S.

There was no running water, electricity, or sewage. Children slept on pieces of cardboard or on tables because their parents, who worked for about eight dollars a day, could not afford to buy them beds.

Everywhere Arthur went, the people of Soweto followed him—especially the children. He taught tennis clinics for them, encouraging children to take up the game and to work for freedom.

By the time he left the country, his visit had inspired millions of South Africans to strive for their rights as human beings.

Top of the World

After his great success in South Africa, Arthur returned to the U.S. at the end of 1973. He had accomplished one of his life's great goals: He had been the first black man to break the color barrier in professional tennis—in the U.S., in Europe and Australia, and now in South Africa.

Even those who had criticized his visit had to admit that the results were worth the trip. South Africa did not gain the benefit of being accepted by the world of sports just because they had let one black man in. But South

African blacks, newly inspired, began struggling even harder for their freedom.

It would take almost twenty more years, but in the end the cruel, racist system of apartheid, or "apartness," was defeated and Nelson Mandela became the country's first black president.

Upon his return Arthur turned his attention back to tennis. Many people felt that at thirty years old, he was past his peak. He hadn't won a grand slam event since the 1970 Australian Open, and the younger generation of players were getting better every year. They were stronger and faster, and hit the ball harder and more accurately than the older players.

Partly this was because tennis had allowed professionals and amateurs to play against one another in major tournaments. Because of this move tennis had become much more popular. Great young athletes took up tennis instead of baseball or basketball. New kinds of physical and mental training gave the younger players a distinct advantage.

But no matter what anyone else thought, Arthur Ashe still believed his best tennis lay ahead of him. The past few years had been full of injuries and distractions, but now he felt ready to make a move up in the rankings.

In 1974 he began to get back into top form. He won only two tournaments that year, but he reached the finals in nine more. By the end of 1974 he had fought his way back to number five in the U.S.

Determined to do even better in the coming year, Arthur began a grueling training program. It was a lot like the training he'd gotten in the army in 1968—and that year had been his greatest on the court.

He began doing better almost immediately. Then in early May he entered the World Championship Tennis (WCT) tournement. Although he suffered from an injury to his heel, he succeeded in beating one of the best young players in the game—Sweden's Björn Borg—in the finals to win the tournament. The prize was a solid gold tennis ball, worth $33,000 at the time.

Arthur decided to skip some of the tournaments right before Wimbledon. Those tournaments were played on clay, a very slow surface that didn't lend itself to Arthur's type of game. Besides, he wanted to let his heel recover.

Winning Wimbledon was something Arthur had dreamed of since his first visit to England while he was still in college at UCLA. He had done well on the fast grass surface, reaching the semifinals more than once, but never coming away with the trophy.

Now he was running out of time, but he felt good about his chances. His confidence was high, and he was healthy and focused.

There was another reason Arthur felt optimistic. He had a plan to win—a surprise change of strategy he'd been considering for a few months. Ever since his college days he'd been a power player, serving hard and running up to the net to volley, catching his opponents back on their heels.

But the younger players, like world number one Jimmy Connors, were too strong and fast and accurate to be beaten that way. If Arthur got into a match with one of them, he would have to change his game completely. Instead of hitting everything hard, he would put as little force as possible into his shots, throwing his opponents off and forcing them into mistakes.

It might not work—he was not used to playing that way and might make mistakes himself—but he felt it was his only hope for victory at Wimbledon.

In the tournaments he'd played in that spring, Arthur did not show off his new strategy; he wanted it to come as a complete surprise. He won the tournament at Beckenham and did well at Nottingham, too, finally losing a close one to Tony Roche, another veteran.

Arthur won his first four matches at Wimbledon. That put him in the final eight, with some of the world's top players left to face.

His next match was against Björn Borg, who was only nineteen at the time. Starting the following year, Borg would win five straight Wimbledon championships and become one of history's immortal tennis players.

But that year he was still young and inexperienced. Arthur had beaten him once before, and he did so again at Wimbledon. After losing the first set and going down three games to none in the second, Arthur rallied to win the match, 2–6, 6–4, 8–6, 6–1.

In the semifinals Arthur's opponent was Tony Roche—the same man who'd beaten him only two weeks earlier. Against Roche, the veteran, Arthur would not be able to take advantage of inexperience. He had to tough it out, using his superb physical conditioning to outlast Roche in five sets: 5–7, 6–4, 7–5, 8–9, 6–4.

He had made it to the finals! But there, he would have to face twenty-three-year-old Jimmy Connors, ranked number one in the world. The Brash Basher was playing at the very top of his game.

The year before, Connors had won the Australian Open, the U.S. Open, Wimbledon, and nine other tournaments. He had won an incredible 96 percent of his matches, and he was doing even better this year. He had breezed through the tournament so far, not losing a single set.

Everyone, from commentators to reporters to fans, was sure Connors would beat Arthur easily. After all, Arthur was almost thirty-two; Connors was nearly ten years younger, stronger, and faster.

The dream of a black man winning Wimbledon, tennis's greatest prize, would have to wait years longer—perhaps generations longer. At least, that was what the world thought.

But not Arthur—he was convinced he could beat Connors.

The night before the match Arthur had dinner with friends and told them his plan for beating Connors. Among them were some of the best minds in tennis. They all agreed Arthur's plan was his best chance for victory.

He went to bed and slept soundly through the night. He was filled with an inner calm. He had a plan, a road to victory. Tomorrow he would follow it to the letter.

He walked onto the court the next morning, made his ceremonial bow to the royal box, and turned to face Jimmy Connors.

Inside his sock Arthur had stuffed a piece of paper with his plan written on it. If he needed to remind himself, he could take it out during a break and look at it. But he didn't think he would need to. The plan was firmly rooted in his mind. Somehow he felt that he could not lose.

Connors was a player who did not like to come to the net. Arthur would force him to do just that. He would hit soft shots, with underspin, that would skid under Connors's racket.

Arthur had never played this way on a grass court. To win the biggest match of his life, he would have to beat Connors not with his physical ability, but with his mind.

It helped that Connors was already angry with Arthur—so angry that he had filed a lawsuit against him. Just a few days before, Arthur had told reporters he thought Connors was unpatriotic because he refused to play for his country on the Davis Cup team. Connors, who considered himself very patriotic, immediately sued Arthur for millions of dollars.

Connors would later quietly withdraw the suit. But at the time of their Wimbledon final it was in full progress. To make Connors even angrier, Arthur wore his red-white-and-blue Davis Cup warm-up jacket onto the court.

Arthur wanted Connors to be as angry as possible—the angrier he was, the more mistakes he was likely to make.

The fans in the stands were cheering hard for Arthur. He had always been a fan favorite, with his perfect manners and his grace and style on the court. They also wanted to see a black man make history. The great Althea Gibson had won Wimbledon in 1957 and 1958, but no black man had ever won the trophy.

As soon as the match began, the crowd began to murmur. It was obvious that Arthur's strategy was working. Connors looked confused on the court. He kept making mistakes. That made him angry, and his anger forced him into even more errors. Within forty-five minutes Arthur had won the first two sets, 6–1, 6–1.

The fans in the stands were shocked. They were glad Arthur was winning, but they wanted Connors at least to make a close match of it. In the third set he did, fighting back with all his might and talent to win the set, 7–5. In the fourth set he jumped out to a 3–0 lead, and it looked as if he might yet rally to defeat Arthur.

As the two men walked to the bench for a scheduled ten-minute break, Arthur could see that his plan was no longer working. He wondered whether he should change back to his normal style of tennis for the rest of the match.

He sat down and took out the piece of paper he'd stuffed into his sock. As he stared at the paper in his hands, everyone in the stands thought he was meditating. But reading over his plan, Arthur felt his confidence return. He would stick with it, no matter what.

When the match resumed, Arthur rallied.

He and Connors traded games until finally Arthur broke Connors's serve. He then went on to win the set, 6–4, and the match.

Then he turned to the stands, where the friends who had helped him come up with his winning strategy were sitting, and raised his fist. It was a gesture of victory and also a reminder of those black Olympic athletes who, in 1968, had done the same thing on the medal stand.

Arthur's Wimbledon victory over Jimmy Connors remains one of tennis's greatest moments. It was among the biggest upsets ever. It showed the way for other players to beat the new breed of power players. And it was, of course, the first time a black man had risen to the very top of the tennis world.

Arthur went on to win seven more tournaments that year, for a total of nine victories. He came in second in five more. His 1975 record was 108–23, for a winning percentage of 82 percent, second best in his career.

At the end of the year he was ranked number one in the U.S. for the first time since 1969. But not only that—for the first time in his life he stood alone at number one in the world!

A New and Bigger Challenge

No black man had ever been ranked the world's best tennis player. Arthur had become the Jackie Robinson of his sport. All over the world young blacks were taking up the "white man's game." Even in South Africa young boys in Soweto pretended to be Arthur Ashe as they smashed the ball across the net.

Once, when he was younger, Arthur would have been unhappy about being the greatest black male tennis player ever. He had wanted to be looked at just like any other top-ranked player. But now he was older and wiser. He knew how important it was for others—particularly young black people—to look up to him.

Three more times in the 1970s he returned to South Africa. He hoped to see it as a free nation someday. In those days it seemed like an impossible dream that Nelson Mandela would ever be freed from the Robben Island prison. No one would have believed he would someday be South Africa's president.

Meanwhile, Arthur continued to play tennis at a high level. He won five tournaments in 1976 and three more in 1977, but that was not good enough to hold on to his number one ranking.

More important to Arthur, he began losing matches to lesser players who could never beat him before. He began to see that he had passed his peak as a champion.

Even so, he hoped he could play on the tour for a few more years before retiring. He felt he could still win big matches, and he still enjoyed the competition.

The Davis Cup continued to be one of his favorites. He played for the U.S. team through the 1978 campaign, compiling a lifetime 27–5 record in cup matches. His twenty-seven victories were the most ever for an American Davis Cup player.

Most important of all during the late 1970s, Arthur met Jeanne Marie Moutoussamy, a young photographer assigned to shoot his portrait. Arthur and Jeanne began dating and were married in New York City on February 20, 1977.

The ceremony was performed by the Reverend Andrew Young, a famous civil rights leader who was then America's ambassador to the United Nations. Arthur, who was recovering from heel surgery at the time, had to hobble down the aisle with his foot in a cast.

After recovering from his surgery, Arthur

returned to action. In 1978 he won three more tournaments. In early 1979 he reached the semifinals of the Australian Open. That earned him an automatic invitation to the 1979 Grand Prix Masters tournament, featuring only the very best players in the game. For a thirty-five-year old, Arthur was still playing very well.

He reached the semifinals easily, then made it to the finals when Jimmy Connors had to bow out because of an injury. Suddenly everyone was buzzing with excitement. Could Arthur really pull off one more miracle?

His opponent in the finals was twenty-year old John McEnroe. McEnroe had just emerged as one of the top players in the world. Later that year he would win his first grand slam tournament, the U.S. Open (he would go on to win the title three years running).

Arthur gave the youngster all he could handle. The crowd gasped as he made shot after incredible shot. Twice Arthur was only one point away from winning the tournament. But McEnroe held off the onslaught and came back to win the match.

Arthur Ashe would never win another tennis tournament. He reached the finals that year in both the U.S. Pro Indoor and the U.S. Indoor Championships but lost both matches.

Then on July 30, 1979, something happened that turned his focus completely away from tennis.

He had just come back to New York from playing in Austria, where he had lost in the second round in what would be the last professional tennis match of his life.

That night as he lay in bed, a sharp pain in his chest forced him to sit straight up, fighting for breath. It went away but came back fifteen minutes later. Again it went away, and once more it returned.

Finally he was able to get back to sleep.

The next morning he went to teach a tennis clinic in the Bronx. In the afternoon he went to another in Queens. There, on a scorching-hot day, he felt the pain return, worse than ever. A doctor who happened to be there looked him over and personally drove him to New York Hospital.

"I want Mr. Ashe admitted as a heart attack patient," he told the orderlies.

Arthur was stunned. He was only thirty-six, and at the peak of physical conditioning. How could he be having a heart attack?

Then he remembered that his mother's death had been caused by early heart disease, added to the strain of her pregnancy. Arthur's father, too, had recently been having heart problems.

At the hospital doctors confirmed that Arthur had suffered a heart attack. He stayed in the hospital for ten days. "If you don't have bypass surgery," they told him, "you'll never be able to play tennis again."

Bypass surgery was pretty new in those days. It meant taking veins from the leg and sewing them into the chest, to bypass the clogged vessels near his heart. It was major surgery, but it was his only hope of ever playing tennis again.

Arthur wasn't sure what to do. Finally, though, he decided to have the operation.

After the surgery Arthur felt better. A week later he was telling friends, "I'll be playing at Wimbledon next June."

Soon he was walking miles every day. A few months later he began running.

But in March 1980, while on vacation with Jeanne in Cairo, Egypt, Arthur felt sharp pains in his chest again.

Doctors diagnosed angina, a condition resulting from blocked blood vessels that causes pain when exercising.

Arthur had to face the truth—there was no getting around it now. He would never play professional tennis again.

On April 16, 1980, he officially retired from the game. "I will now begin a new season," he said, "of writing, talking, listening, and assisting."

There were many things he still wanted to do—things he had put off while he was still playing tennis. Now he would have time for new challenges.

Life After Tennis

In his tennis career Arthur Ashe Jr. had won three out of the four grand slam tournaments— the U.S. Open, the Australian Open, and Wimbledon. He'd won the doubles title at the fourth, the French Open, and at the Australian Open. He had won thirty-three events in his twelve-year career.

Perhaps even more important was the way in which he had won—with elegant style, amazing grace, and the manners of a perfect gentleman. He beat better players because he was able to conquer them with his mind.

For blacks he had been an inspiration. For fans both black and white he was someone they could welcome into their hearts.

Because of all this he was now in a position to do many exciting things with the rest of his life. Arthur wanted to speak out in public on issues he cared about, such as equal rights for blacks in America and South Africa. He also began working with the American Heart Association to promote heart health and with the United Negro College Fund. He helped young people in cities get involved with tennis and improve their grades. He began working as a part-time TV commentator for tennis events.

Arthur wanted to do some writing, too. He had already written two autobiographies, with the help of professional writers: *Advantage Ashe* in 1967, and *Arthur Ashe: Portrait in Motion* in 1975. In 1976 he'd contributed to a book called *Mastering Your Tennis Strokes*.

Now he wrote articles for *Tennis* magazine, a tennis column in the *Washington Post,* and another memoir, *Off the Court*, published in 1981.

Arthur had even bigger ambitions as a writer, but those would have to wait. In 1981 he was invited to serve as the coach, or "captain," of the American Davis Cup team. Arthur, who had always loved competing for his country, eagerly accepted.

That year the Americans looked very strong. Jimmy Connors was on the team, and so was John McEnroe. Their chances of recapturing the cup seemed excellent.

But it would not be as easy as it seemed. Connors had finally decided to join the team, six years after Arthur had scolded him about it at Wimbledon. But he was not happy about it—Davis Cup matches took time away from moneymaking tennis tournaments and commercial contracts.

In fact, Connors was so unhappy that after

winning his first two matches, he left the team and did not return until 1984, three years later.

Still, the team remained strong without him—strong enough to win the Davis Cup that year, and the following year too.

In 1983 things did not go as well. The U.S. had to play low-ranked Argentina in the first round. The Argentines were a much better team than their ranking because the year before they had lost in the first round. On top of that, they would be playing at home, on clay, a surface that favored them. Finally, it was summer in Argentina, and the weather was terribly hot.

In the end the Argentines crushed the U.S., 4–1. It was a big disappointment to Arthur. But there were worse things to come.

In June of that year Arthur had to return to the hospital for a second heart operation—a double bypass this time.

After the surgery Arthur felt weak, and his

doctors suggested a blood transfusion to build up his strength and help him recover faster. Arthur agreed to receive the blood, and soon afterward he began to feel better.

By 1984's Davis Cup season Arthur was at full strength again. And there was good news—Jimmy Connors had rejoined the team.

Or was it good news? Now instead of one brash, badly behaved young millionaire superstar to coach, Arthur would have *two*—Connors and McEnroc.

Both players refused to listen to Arthur's coaching advice. Connors still perhaps carried a grudge over Arthur's calling him unpatriotic.

And in 1981 Arthur had publicly scolded McEnroe for cursing at a referee, calling his behavior "disgraceful." To curse at an official in a professional tournament was embarrassing for their sport, Arthur felt. To do it in a Davis Cup match was a disgrace to their country as well.

Arthur did not want to cause a fight by

scolding the two players this time. He felt that would be bad for the team. They were winning, breezing through their first three matches, and he did not want to upset his players before the finals against Sweden.

The Swedes had a strong team, but the Americans were heavily favored. McEnroe was so confident that he showed up for practice only four days before the match.

Arthur was worried, and he turned out to be right. The underdog Swedes surprised the American squad, defeating them to win the cup.

Now there was grumbling among the players. They blamed Arthur for their failure, saying he hadn't given them any coaching or advice.

Arthur knew his days as Davis Cup coach were numbered. He had done the best he could in a difficult situation, where those he was supposed to coach were more powerful than he was.

Still, his firing in 1985 came as a bitter disappointment. Happily, that same year he was voted into the Tennis Hall of Fame, honoring his achievements both as a player and as Davis Cup captain.

With more free time, Arthur threw himself back into his off-the-court activities. Over the next three years he wrote a three-volume history of black athletes in America, *A Hard Road to Glory*, which has become a classic and which must be counted as one of his greatest achievements.

In 1986 Arthur and Jeanne achieved something even greater—their daughter, Camera, was born. Arthur, who had always been shy and reserved—some even said cold—lavished affection and love on his baby daughter. As a man with serious heart problems, he knew he could not count on always being there for her.

He was right. The following year he was operated on for a rare brain infection.

Doctors grew suspicious and ran some blood tests. What they found came as a shock to Arthur and Jeanne.

Somehow Arthur had contracted a deadly disease for which there was no cure—AIDS.

Miles to Go
Before I Sleep

The news came as a devastating blow to Arthur and Jeanne. They could not understand at first how he could have gotten AIDS, which most people get from taking drugs or doing other risky things. But Arthur had never taken drugs. And he was a faithful husband.

Then the doctors explained that the blood transfusion they had given him after his second operation was infected with the HIV virus that causes AIDS. It had taken five years, but the virus was now strong inside him. He was in very delicate health.

Arthur and Jeanne knew that if the world found out he had AIDS, they would never have any privacy again. They decided to hide his illness for as long as possible so that they could continue to live full, normal lives.

He might not have many years left, but this way Arthur could spend lots of time with Jeanne and with their daughter, Camera, the new love of his life.

So they carried on as if everything were fine. They were vacationing at their home in Florida that winter when the news came that Arthur's father had died.

Arthur cried and cried. The man he loved most in the world was dead. The man who had sacrificed so much for his boys, who had brought them up without a mother but still managed to teach them such strong values, was no more.

In his father's death Arthur could see a preview of his own. He held his daughter tightly, praying that he would live long enough to see her grow up.

He knew, though, that this was not likely to happen. Just as he had lost his own mother too soon, Camera would probably lose him.

So he began writing another memoir, *Days of Grace*, which he continued to work on for the rest of his life. As part of the book he wrote a long chapter as his last letter to Camera. In it he told her all about what he'd tried to do in life, the guiding principles he had lived by and hoped she would live by too.

He felt better knowing that when he was gone, at least she would have the letter to guide her.

In those years when they kept his awful secret, Arthur did not stop his activities in the world, even if he did have to slow down a bit. He was arrested twice while marching against America's treatment of black refugees from Haiti.

He returned to South Africa one last time

in 1991, to find the country transformed. Nelson Mandela was now the president, and its system of racist laws was no more. To Arthur, it was like a miracle.

Finally, in April 1992, rumors about his illness began to spread. Fearing the story would appear in the newspapers if he did not say anything, Arthur decided to break the news to the world himself. In a shaking voice he announced at a news conference that he had AIDS.

Several months earlier basketball star Magic Johnson had made the same announcement. AIDS was emerging as a disease that anybody could get. People were frightened, and they began to demand that the government support the search for a cure.

Immediately Arthur threw himself into AIDS activism. He founded his own organization to help find a cure. And he still worked with African-American teens, helping them compete in sports and finish high school.

AIDS is a disease that robs people of their ability to fight infections. It doesn't show its face when they are healthy. But once they get sick, it is hard for them to recover. Arthur could only try to stay healthy for as long as possible, in the hope that a cure would be found in time to help him.

He knew, though, that his chances weren't good. He had been infected almost ten years earlier—the average time it took for AIDS to kill. He needed to make every moment count.

The family's Christmas vacation that year turned out to be their last together. Shortly after that, in January 1993, Arthur fell ill with a rare form of pneumonia that is all too common in AIDS patients. He was rushed to the hospital, but he kept getting sicker.

Friends and family came to visit by the dozens. Then one day Arthur received a visit from a friend he had never met in person— Nelson Mandela. Their time together was

one of the high points of Arthur's life, and of Mandela's, too.

On February 6 Arthur Ashe Jr. died with his family by his side. He was only forty-nine years old.

The tennis world went into mourning. His millions of fans around the globe were shocked and saddened. They had loved him for more than just his superb skill at tennis. It was his courage and caring they loved the most.

Arthur had inspired millions to do better, to care more, and to work harder to change the world. In death, as in life, he was a model for young people, especially blacks.

"Whatever it is, you can do it," was the message they took from him.

Richmond—the city where he'd been born, where he'd grown up, and where he'd learned about injustice—decided to honor Arthur by having his body lie in state at the state capitol. He was the first man so honored since

Confederate general Stonewall Jackson.

Years later Richmond also honored Arthur with a statue. If you go there today and ride down the boulevard past the statues of Confederate generals from the Civil War, you will see a statue that doesn't belong among them—a statue of a young black man holding a tennis racket. The plaque below the statue reads ARTHUR ASHE JR.—1943–1993.

For More Information

BOOKS

Ashe, Arthur, Jr. *Advantage Ashe.* With Clifford George Gewecke Jr. New York: Coward-McCann, 1967.

Arthur Ashe, Portrait in Motion: A Diary. With Frank Deford. Boston: Houghton Mifflin, 1975. Reprint, with an introduction by Frank Deford. New York: Carroll and Graf Publishers/Richard Gallen, 1993.

Arthur Ashe's Tennis Clinic. New York: Simon and Schuster, 1981.

A Hard Road to Glory: A History of the African-American Athlete, 1919–1945.

With Kip Branch, Ocania Chalk, and
Francis Harris. New York: Warner
Books, 1988.

Off the Court. With Neil Amdur. New York:
New American Library, 1981.

Ashe, Arthur, Jr. and Arnold Rampersad.
Days of Grace: A Memoir. New York:
Alfred A. Knopf, 1993.

Dexter, Robin. *Young Arthur Ashe: Brave
Champion.* Mahwah, N.J.: Troll
Associates, 1996.

Robinson, Louie. *Arthur Ashe, Tennis
Champion.* Garden City, N.Y.:
Doubleday, 1967.

Weissberg, Ted. *Arthur Ashe.* Los Angeles:
Melrose Square Publishing, 1993.

VIDEOS

Arthur Ashe: Citizen of the World. VHS. Directed by Julie Anderson. HBO Sports/HBO Home Video, 1994.

Play Better Tennis. Vol. 1, *The Fundamentals.* VHS. Starring Arthur Ashe. 1985.

Play Better Tennis. Vol. 2, *Advanced Techniques.* VHS. Starring Arthur Ashe. 1985.

Tennis Our Way. VHS. Starring Arthur Ashe and Stan Smith. Republic Studios, 1986.